Here is a list of things
people have said about Nina Soni.

"Nina Soni is many things: Indian American, a list-maker, a word-definer, and a big sister. She is funny, observant, and smart, and she can also sometimes be a bit forgetful. The number one thing that Nina is? Loveable! I adore Nina and know readers will, too."

—Debbi Michiko Florence, author of
the Jasmine Toguchi series

"A perfect fit for readers who enjoy realistic fiction about friendship and self-discovery."

—*School Library Journal*

"…a flawed but refreshing and very likable protagonist…"

—*Booklist*

"A sweet and entertaining series opener about family and friendship."

—*Kirkus Reviews*

She's a phenomenon!

Phe-no-me-non means a happening or an event.

In loving memory of Pearl Jabs, who was a
third grandmother to my daughters

—K. S.

Published by
PEACHTREE PUBLISHING COMPANY INC.
1700 Chattahoochee Avenue
Atlanta, Georgia 30318-2112
PeachtreeBooks.com

Edited by Kathy Landwehr
Design and composition by Adela Pons
The illustrations were rendered digitally.

Printed and bound in August 2022 at Lake Book Manufacturing, Melrose Park, IL, USA
10 9 8 7 6 5 4 3 2 1 (hardcover)
10 9 8 7 6 5 4 3 2 1 (paperback)
First Edition
HC ISBN: 978-1-68263-498-1
PB ISBN: 978-1-68263-499-8

Cataloging-in-Publication Data is available from the Library of Congress.

NINA SONI

SNOW SPY

Written by **Kashmira Sheth**
Illustrated by **Jenn Kocsmiersky**

PEACHTREE
ATLANTA

CHAPTER ONE

"Nina, have you heard of any grand songwriters?" my sister Kavita asked on our way to school.

I caught a snowflake on my tongue. "There're a lot of great songwriters."

"Has anyone written a grand song about snow?" Kavita wanted to know.

Yesterday she had asked me if "grand" was a "grand" word. I had said yes, so today she was using it. Kavita is in first grade, and she wonders about a lot of strange things, including words. I am in fourth grade, and she expects me to have all the answers.

Ex-pect means to believe that something you want or ask for will be given to you.

"How about 'Let It Snow!'? And don't forget 'Dashing through the snow,' from 'Jingle Bells,'" I said. "I'm sure there are a lot more."

"But not a grand one."

I inspected a giant snowflake that landed on my sleeve. "How do you know that?"

"If there was one, I would be singing it." She picked up a stick. "When I make up a snow song, it will be grand. You know why?"

"Yes," I replied. "Kavita means 'poetry,' and that is why you love to make up songs and sing them."

"Yup!" She threw the stick as far as she could. "Mine will be the best. I might even get a prize for it."

"You might."

Just then Jay came out of his house. He lives on my street, he's in my class, and he's my best friend. I waved at him.

Kavita tugged my jacket. "Will you listen to my song, Nina?"

"When it's ready, I will."

Jay joined us. "Hey."

"Jay, did you know your name rhymes with 'hey'?" Kavita sang as we all walked along, *"Hey, hey, hey! Horses eat hey!"*

She was mixing up "hey" with "hay."

I explained. "Kavita, the hay that horses eat is spelled *h-a-y*. The greeting kind of 'hey' is spelled *h-e-y*."

She looked confused. "But they sound the same."

"Yes, they do," I said. "When two words sound the same but are spelled differently and mean different things, they're called homophones. Like 'I'—meaning 'you'—and 'eye' like the eyes on your face."

Kavita was quiet. Jay lifted his eyebrows at me. We were both surprised by her silence.

Finally she asked, "What is that word called again?"

"Homophone," Jay and I both said at the same time.

"Kavita, thanks for letting me know what rhymes with my name," he added.

"You're welcome." Kavita asked, "Did you know I'm working on a grand snow song?"

"That's nice." Jay knows Kavita as well as I do. It's good because I never have to explain to him how peculiar Kavita can be, how she makes up songs and sings them, how weird her questions can be.

Pe-cu-liar means something or someone who is different and kind of strange.

"I was wondering if you'd like to come over sometime during the long weekend," I said to Jay. "I haven't asked my parents, but I'm sure they'll say yes."

"Jeff and Nora are coming tonight and we're going skiing tomorrow. They'll be here until Sunday evening. How about Monday?"

Jeff and Nora are Jay's cousins. They both live close by and visit him all the time. The three of them do a lot of things together. Especially on weekends.

"Yes, come on Monday," I said.

A gust of wind came and shook the branch above us. We got snow-showered.

"Isn't snow awesome?" Jay asked.

"Snow is awesome. Snow is soft. Snow is light. Snow is bright," Kavita sang. I guess this was part of Kavita's grand snow song!

"Do you really think snow is awesome, or do you think it's awesome because you're going skiing?" I asked Jay.

"Nina, what's the difference?"

"There's a big difference. If you think snow is awesome, then it means you like how it feels as it comes down, so fluffy and soft. Or maybe you think it's amazing that each flake is a different shape. Or maybe you like the fact that snow is basically water but in a different form. Any of these would mean that you are truly in awe of snow."

"And if I think it's awesome because I'm going skiing?"

Kavita had stopped singing and was paying attention to us.

"Then you want a fresh layer to ski on that's all smooth and even, not icy and bumpy. That means you're just thinking what snow can do for you and missing the magic."

"What are you saying, Nina?" Kavita asked.

Before I could answer, Jay added, "And why are you saying it?"

I let out a big white breath. I watched it curl up, up and away. The reason I was going after Jay was because I was jealous of all the plans he had for the weekend. I didn't want to admit that. "Kavita, I was just trying to find out why Jay really likes snow."

She pointed at the snowflakes. "Because they dance as they come down."

"Awesome answer, Kavita!" Jay said. Then he asked, "Are you doing anything special this weekend?"

"Hey, don't change the subject," I said.

"It's the same topic." He shrugged. "We're still discussing the weekend."

I sighed. "We don't have any plans." And then I remembered. "Actually, we're having guests."

"They're going to stay over for two nights," Kavita added.

Jay didn't seem to believe us. "Who's coming?"

"My parents' friend from college and his family. Their daughter Priya is my age, and their son Nayan is little younger than Kavita."

"Oh yeah?" Jay's green eyes filled with surprise. "How come you never mentioned them before?"

Maybe Jay was secretly unhappy. He never seems jealous. Usually I'm the one who's not happy about him spending so much time with his cousins and grandpa. Now things had turned around. I liked it.

By then we were at school, and Kavita ran to the playground. "Yay for Priya and Nayan!"

"They just moved to Wisconsin," I told Jay as we headed toward the door.

"That means you've never met them before, right?"

Jay was probably thinking that they were strangers and that we may not like them. "So what? We will have fun," I said as we hung our jackets in our cubbies.

We entered the classroom. "I hope so. Two days and nights is a long time if you don't like them," he teased.

✳✳✳

Sometimes I am bored at school. It's not because we don't have challenging work to do; it's because we have to do certain things in the same order every day. One class is stacked upon another. Right after homeroom there is language arts, then social studies, then math, and finally recess. After recess there is PE or music then science.

Except for at school, I like things stacked up and organized better than I like things scattered all around the place. I really do. That's why I make lists in my notebook. I call my notebook Sakhi.

> Sakhi means friend in Hindi.

I know Hindi because my parents speak in Hindi with each other, their Indian friends, and when they talk on the phone to our family in India. Kavita and I can only speak a little Hindi with our parents and grandparents, but we understand more of it. Sometimes Kavita and I say things in Hindi to each other when we are outside our home and don't want anyone else to know what we're saying. Then Hindi becomes our secret language.

Even though my notebook has a Hindi name, I make my lists in English. That is because the Hindi alphabet is different from the English one. My name in English is written "Nina." In Hindi it is written "नीना."

Having Sakhi to write down lists in is an advantage.

Ad-van-tage means all the good stuff that comes out of something. That good stuff can be very useful or help you in some way.

In-my-head list of list-making advantages

✱ Like a neat stack of books, a list keeps thoughts tidy.

* Each item on a list is only one or two lines and not as long as a book.
* That means it doesn't take much time to make a list.
* It also doesn't take much time to review a list.
* Because a list is tidy, it is easy to pick a task or focus on something from a list.

While I was bored earlier today, I made a list of the fun we might have this weekend. It was already Friday, so I think it was fine to daydream about it. I mean, Friday is practically the weekend. And since we would also have Monday off from school, this was a special weekend, even if we weren't going skiing.

In-my-head list of super-special long-weekend fun

* I'll have a new friend to play with.

* Kavita will have her own new friend, so she won't be bothering me and Priya.

* Mom and Dad will also have old friends to be with. They really like old friends.

* We will have yummy food.

* Priya and I might get to stay up late.

* Maybe the four of us kids can do something special together, like Jay does with his cousins.

I couldn't wait for school to end. Unfortunately, it was only nine in the morning, and we had to stay here all day. I looked out the window. The snow had started to fall faster and faster.

Wouldn't it be fun if Kavita, Priya, Nayan, and I could build a giant snowman and have a snowball fight? Maybe even build a snow fort?

A snow fort!

Kavita and I had never made one before.

I made an in-my-head list of the things we could do in a snow fort.

* We could play in it.

* We could have snack in it.

* We could have secret talks in it.

* No one could see us or hear us while we were in it, so we could watch everything and everyone.

* Maybe we could keep an eye on our neighborhood.

* Maybe we could be spies.

Snow Spies!

The snow spy idea was exciting. Usually nothing much happens on our street, but maybe something interesting would this weekend. I crossed my fingers to make my weekend wish come true.

"Nina," Ms. Lapin called.

I looked up. "I'm sorry," I said. I know daydreaming is not allowed in a classroom. I don't ever plan to do it, it just happens. Like now. I wonder if that's why it is called "daydreaming." It's just like a night dream but it pops in your brain during the day. I daydream a lot and usually don't get caught. But today I was not so lucky.

Ms. Lapin said, "Please start reading where Kyle left off."

The book was open in front of me. We were reading a story that I liked, but I had lost track of where we were. I picked up the book but had no idea where to begin. Ms. Lapin's eyes were on me. Someone coughed. Ms. Lapin glanced away to see who it was.

"Chapter four, page eighteen, top of the page," Jay whispered.

I quickly flipped to page eighteen and started reading.

Sometimes it helps to have your best friend sitting next to you in the classroom.

I knew I was lucky to have Jay in my class. Maybe I shouldn't be jealous of him. Maybe I should be a better friend to him.

***

At lunch I told Megan about my plans for Priya and Nayan's visit. Megan and I are in different classes, but we have the same lunch break. I always sit with her, and we both bring lunch from home. Jay usually buys lunch and eats with Tyler.

Megan opened her lunch box. "I think you'll have enough snow for a snow fort. You and Kavita will just have to convince Priya and Nayan to help you build it and spy with you."

"You think they may not want to?" Before she could answer, I listed all the reasons they might say no to me. "They might not like the cold. They might hate snow. They might want to stay in the warm house." I sighed and took a bite of my chutney and cucumber sandwich.

"I hope not!" Megan pointed to the window. Large

fluffy snowflakes were floating down. "Look at that! How can anyone not like snow?" Then she picked up an apple.

The cilantro and mint chutney tasted like summer. For a moment I had almost forgotten the magic of snow. "You are right. As long as we're prepared and warm, it'd be fun. I will make sure we bundle up before going out. And we will take a hot cocoa break to warm up."

"Yup. Your plan will be a lot more exciting than sitting inside playing board games all weekend." Megan was quiet for a moment. "Hope they have the right kinds of coats and mittens."

"I'm sure they do, because they have been going to school here," I said. "What are you doing this weekend?"

Megan crunched her apple. I waited.

She took a gulp of milk before saying, "My mom says it's a surprise. I think we might be going to my uncle's farm."

"You go to your uncle's house all the time. What would be so special about it this time?"

"I don't know." Megan shook her head. "I've been trying to find out."

"You mean you're spying?" I ate the last of my sandwich.

"Yes. Without being a Snow Spy."

For the rest of the day, I really tried to pay attention. Not to my thoughts in my brain, but to what Ms. Lapin was saying in the classroom. I didn't want to get caught daydreaming again.

It seemed like the day was a sledding hill. I was climbing up and up, but I hadn't reached the top.

***

By the time Kavita, Jay, and I walked home from school, snow had covered the streets, roofs, and trees.

Some of the sidewalks were shoveled but not all. There were rabbit and squirrel tracks in a couple of front yards. Maybe we could spy on animals over the weekend. Would that be considered spying?

I love trudging through the fresh snow because you can feel your boots sinking down, down, down. Then you have to lift your legs up, up, up. It's hard work, but I don't mind.

Finally, we reached our street. Jay waved goodbye and walked toward his house.

We have a clump of spruce trees on the north side of the house. Since they're evergreen, they keep their needles all winter long. Today their green branches were dusted with snow like powdered sugar on a doughnut. They looked delicious enough to eat. Not that I tried to eat them or anything.

Mom stood at the window waiting for us. In good weather she waits right outside the front door, and in cold weather she stays at the bay window. She looks anxious if Kavita and I are late. Today we were on time.

But she had worried lines on her forehead as she waved to us, the type of lines Kavita draws on her stick people's big faces. She draws three lines, and they take up all the room on a person's forehead.

Even though Kavita and I were excited about having guests, I wondered if maybe Mom wasn't happy. Maybe she was nervous about having people stay at our house.

It meant more work for her and Dad. They had to cook, clean, and entertain.

En-ter-tain means to make sure someone you invite doesn't get bored at your house or at your party.

As soon as we went in the house, I took off my hat, jacket, and mittens. Mom helped Kavita hang up her coat.

"When are Priya and Nayan going to be here?" I asked.

"Tomorrow around ten or eleven," Mom replied.

"Yippee!" said Kavita.

Mom still wore that worried look.

"Mom, do you like Sanjay Uncle and Rita Auntie?" I asked.

"Very much. Why?"

I shrugged. "I thought you looked upset."

"I'm looking forward to seeing them." She smiled.

I felt better.

Mom pointed to the counter. "Your snack is ready so please wash your hands." Her phone rang. "Nina, can you get milk for both of you?" she asked before answering the call.

I nodded.

"We should make a snow fort this weekend," I said to Kavita as I poured milk for us. I handed her a glass.

Kavita took a sip of her milk. "I don't know how. Have you made one before?"

"No." I put the milk jug back in the refrigerator. "That's why we should do it. With Priya and Nayan there will be four of us. More of us means we can get more work done. We could make a very big, sturdy fort. We can play inside, hide, and even spy from in there. Wouldn't that be fun?"

"It isn't nice to spy on our friends and neighbors, Nina."

Kavita was right. "Maybe someone else will show up and we can spy on them."

She sang out loud, *"Snow fort, big and sturdy. Snow fort, white and dazzly."*

And I whispered to myself, *"Snow fort, snow fort, for Nina Soni, Snow Spy!"*

CHAPTER TWO

"Please get your homework done before Priya and Nayan come," Mom said while we ate our snack.

I took a sip of milk. "I only had one thing and I finished it at school."

Kavita spread peanut butter on her apple slice. "No homework, no schoolwork, no nothing to get done!"

"Mom, after we finish eating, can we go play in the snow?" I asked.

"Did you both clean up your rooms like I asked you to?"

Oops, I had forgotten to do that. Mom had told me to tidy up my room last week, but I procrastinated.

Pro-cras-ti-nate means not to do things right away. It is like the game kick the can. You kick the job you are supposed to do to the next day or the next week.

Now I had to pick up that can. I mean pick up that room.

Kavita shook her head. "I don't know how to clean."

"Put all the toys in the toy chest. Gather up your dirty clothes and pile them in the laundry basket. Then make your bed," Mom said.

"It's too hard to make my bed," Kavita whined.

"Try to smooth out your sheet, then your blanket, and then the quilt. I will vacuum both your rooms," Mom said.

"Thanks!" Kavita and I both said at the same time and ran upstairs.

I opened my door and stared. Five days a week I am in school. Even when I am at home, I spend a lot of time downstairs with my family. Who knew sleeping, changing clothes, and doing homework could be so untidy!

More than anything I wondered why hadn't I cleaned earlier?

In-my-head list of why I had procrastinated

* What if I had cleaned my room too early and it got messy again? Then I would have to do it all over again.

* What if our guests canceled their visit? Then my cleaning work would be done for no good reason.

* The same thing could happen if Mom, Dad, Kavita, or I got sick and asked our guests not to come—wasted cleaning.

* If I cleaned up my room I would get used to a perfect room and then when it got messy again, I wouldn't like it.

* Then I would have to keep my room clean for the rest of my life.

* The rest of my life is a long time. It would mean doing a lot of work for as long as I live.

* I am just a kid, and I should spend my time playing and learning, sleeping and eating, and laughing and making lists. Not picking up and cleaning up and prettying up my room.

None of those excuses would work with Mom, though.

I sighed, then got going.

First, I gathered the clothes from the floor, under the bed, on top of the bed, and on the back of my chair. I put them in a laundry basket. Some of them may have been clean, but I didn't want to look or smell each one to figure out which were dirty or smelly. One more wash was the easiest thing to do.

Now that my bed didn't have any clothes on it, I could make it.

Finally, I tackled my desk. I plopped all the pencils and pens in a holder, stacked up books and notebooks into two separate piles, and wiped the tabletop.

I heard Mom vacuuming. I wondered if she had helped Kavita pick up her mess. If only I had spied on them, I would know!

It really was amazing how much I could get done if I put my mind to it. Mom asked me to do it and I couldn't get out of it. So I had no choice, but I was still impressed with all I accomplished.

Ac-com-plished means something you got done very nicely.

Usually it is difficult for me to focus on one thing. My mind has many tracks, and my ideas are like trains. I go down a track chasing one idea, but then a new one comes along. That's when I forget the old idea and go after the new one. On and on it keeps going, with more and more new ideas. To get my chores done, I had to close off all other tracks except the one about cleaning my room. And I did it!

By now, Mom had finished in Kavita's room and was vacuuming the hallway. I got up on the bed so she could go over every inch of my room.

When she was done, Mom looked around. "Doesn't your room look bigger when it is clean?"

"It does. I wish I could keep it this way all the time."

Mom smiled. "That's difficult, but you can try. Every day after you finish your homework you can spend five minutes picking up things."

"Only five minutes? I spent more than twenty minutes today!"

"When was the last time you cleaned your room, Nina?"

I tried to remember but could not. "A long time ago."

"If you do it every day, picking up will not take much time and your room will be nicer."

Mom was right. It would be easy to do, but I thought of other problems with keeping my room tidy.

In-my-head list of keeping-my-room-tidy problems

* I would have to pick up every single day.
* It would be hard to remember to do that.
* I am usually in a hurry to finish my homework so I can do other things.
* If the other thing is "picking up my room," I may not want to finish my homework.

* That means not only would my room stay messy, but my homework would stay unfinished.

* Then I would end up with bad grades.

Mom sat next to me on the bed. "What are you thinking, Nina?"

I didn't tell Mom that if I tried to keep my room clean, I might get in trouble for not finishing my homework and getting bad grades, and I'd still have a messy room. "Mom, I want to, but I don't think I can pick up every day."

Mom ran her fingers through my hair. "You can try. But don't worry about it."

Kavita came in. "Are you ready, Nina?"

I had forgotten about going out. "Mom, can Kavita and I play in the snow now?"

"It will get dark soon, so stay close to the kitchen window. That way I can keep an eye on you," Mom said.

"OK."

We all went downstairs. Mom started cooking and Kavita and I bundled up.

What I like about snow at night is, it reflects the street-light, and the glow keeps everything shimmering. The night never gets very dark.

"Let's get started on the snow fort. Roll the snowballs and bring them to me," I said to Kavita.

"Why do I have to bring them to you?" Kavita asked. "Can't you just build next to me?"

"I guess."

We started to gather snow. It was a challenge because we were supposed to stay by the window and there wasn't much snow there. We rolled a few balls. *Where should we build the fort?* I wondered.

To find the perfect location for the fort, I had to survey the whole yard.

Sur-vey means to think about a project and figure out the best way to go about doing it.

It is not easy to survey when you are supposed to stay close to one place.

"Let's see if Jay is outside," Kavita said.

It would be fun to see what Jay, Jeff, and Nora were doing. But for that we would have to walk to the front yard. "We can't do that. Mom wants us to stay by the kitchen window," I reminded Kavita.

"We won't go far. Only to our curb."

Just then a car came down our street. A car we had never seen before. Kavita and I watched as it turned into our neighbors' driveway. Mr. and Mrs. Crump had left for Arizona today, so who was here?

"Do you know who that is?" Kavita asked me.

"No," I whispered.

The person stayed in the car. It wasn't very late, but in winter the sun sets early. Even with the streetlights reflecting off the snow, we couldn't get a good look at the driver.

Maybe Mr. Crump had come back because of something important. But he has a white car. This one was blue.

"Let's go find out who it is," Kavita said.

I grabbed her hand and held it tight.

"Chupke se," I said in Hindi because I didn't want the person in the car to understand that I was telling Kavita to be quiet.

"You mean it could be someone who is here to steal from Mr. and Mrs. Crump?" Kavita whispered.

I thought we would be spying for fun. Now I wasn't sure. Could this be real? Maybe even dangerous? My heart was beating fast.

The car door opened.

We stayed close to the kitchen window but moved behind the spruce clump. It hid us from the person in the car. Someone tall got out. Taller than Mrs. Crump and much younger than her or Mr. Crump.

"It's not Mr. or Mrs. Crump for sure." This time Kavita didn't whisper.

"Chupke se." Again I reminded her to be quiet.

We watched the mystery person open the mailbox.

Mystery person took the mail, got back into the car, and drove away.

"Now the person's gone, and we can't follow because we're just kids," Kavita said.

"You're right about not following. We have to stay safe." I made an in-my-head list.

* We don't know if the person who took the mail is a man or a woman.

* Maybe we should call the suspect Mystery Person. MP for short.

* MP might return tomorrow.

* If we build a snow fort, we can keep an eye on our neighbors' house from a safe hiding place.

"Let's focus on the fort now and worry about MP later," I said.

"The name of the person who took the Crumps' mail is MP?"

"No, and it may not be a man, it might be a woman."
I packed down a snowball. "We can call the mail thief
Mystery Person, MP for short."

"I like that name."

We made a few more snowballs.

Kavita got up. "There is not enough snow by the window. No snow, no fun."

"We haven't done much, Kavita," I said.

"I know, but I have to pee." She clapped her mittened
hands to shake off the snow dust. Kavita sang, *"Let it snow,
let it snow, all night long. Let us build, let us build, all day
long."*

She walked toward the house.

I looked at my snowballs. They were small. Kavita was
right. If it snowed all night, there would be tons of it in the
morning. And if we didn't have to stay by the window, we
would have more snow to make huge snowballs.

Kavita opened the door.

What if MP returned? I didn't want to be outside alone.
I followed Kavita. "I'm coming in too."

Inside, Kavita and I set the table for dinner. Dad roasted thin lentil wafers. Mom was humming softly as she garnished dal soup with cilantro. I thought maybe Dad had said something to cheer her up.

"Mom, you look happy now," I said.

"I am."

"Were you worried about something before?" I asked.

"Yes." She turned to look at me. "I was nervous about a project but the deadline has been pushed back. Now I can enjoy the weekend with our friends and have plenty of time to finish it after they leave."

It felt good to be in the warm kitchen, close to the whole happy family.

Then I thought about MP. "When are the Crumps coming back, Dad?" I asked.

He put the rice on the table. "Not for a couple of months."

"Did they ask us to pick up their mail like they usually do?"

"No. I'm sure they're having it forwarded since they'll be gone for so long."

I bit my nail. I usually don't do that. I guess this was serious, not usual, if I was acting out of the ordinary.

If I had Sakhi with me, I would have made a list in it. Sakhi was upstairs and dinner was ready. I made another in-my-head list.

* If the Crumps had forwarded their mail, why was there mail in their mailbox?
* Who was this MP?
* Why did MP take the Crumps' mail?
* Should I tell Mom and Dad about it?

But I didn't tell Mom and Dad. I stayed quiet. This was my chance to be a real Snow Spy and identify Mystery Person.

I-den-ti-fy means to find out who the person, plant, animal, or thing really is.

I was going to figure out who this MP was and what MP wanted. It was a big job but maybe Priya would want to help me with it. Together we could be successful Snow Spies.

CHAPTER THREE

Snow-covered roofs! That's what I saw when I looked out my window the next morning.

I rushed downstairs.

"Good morning, Mom."

"Good morning, Nina," she said, closing the dishwasher.

I slid by her and went to the kitchen door. Through the foggy glass panel, I could see the spruce trees. Their branches hung low with the weight of the snow, and the maple limbs nearby were white on the top and brown on the bottom. Only a few flakes were lazily floating down now.

"Does the snow remind you of your childhood, Mom?" I asked.

She came closer and rested her hands on my shoulders to look out the window with me. "The beautiful snow does remind me of my childhood," she said dreamily. "Except there're no Himalayan mountains here."

I tilted my head to look at her. "Do you miss them?"

"Yes." Today she had a sad look, not a worried one like yesterday.

"Maybe someday we can travel to your hometown."

Mom twirled me around. "Sure!" She kissed the top of my head. "I haven't been back there in more than ten years! It would be wonderful for all of us to visit together."

It felt so good to make Mom happy!

Dad came in rubbing his palms. "I can't wait. Sanjay and Rita will be here in a couple of hours." He smiled from ear to ear, just the way Kavita draws her smiling people. He was in an excellent mood.

Ex-cel-lent means something that is first-class. Like the top of the heap.

"Don't forget Priya and Nayan," I said.

"Who are they?" Dad tried to look puzzled, but he didn't fool me.

"You know who they are!"

He laughed. "The snow has almost stopped. Right after I drink my tea, I'll clean the driveway."

"I'll help you," Mom said. "I think we have had about six inches."

"That much?" His face fell. "I hope the roads are ploughed."

I love snow and more snow meant more fun. But now Dad was worried whether our guests would be able to visit. They had moved from Florida to Wisconsin only a few months ago. Were they prepared for driving in our Wisconsin winter weather?

What if they couldn't come at all? All my daydreaming at school would be wasted.

I tried to shovel that worrisome thought right out of my brain. I didn't want my daydream to turn into a day-mare. (Is "daymare" a word? If not, it should be!)

I wanted enough snow for the fort but not so much that our guests couldn't get here. I crossed my fingers.

***

After breakfast, we all went outside. By that time, it had stopped snowing. We had a mountain of snow. Well, not really a mountain, but we certainly had a lot.

Usually Dad clears the snow by himself. Sometimes Mom or I help him. I don't say Kavita helps because she usually just plays outside. But this time we all worked. Dad used the snowblower to clear our driveway while the rest of us shoveled the sidewalk.

Our house is on a corner, so we have twice as much sidewalk as our neighbors. On top of that, we cleared the Crumps' sidewalk too. We shoveled and then shoveled some more.

Only two other neighbors were outside cleaning their snow. The noise of our snowblower was too loud for talking, so we just waved at them.

I looked for Mystery Person's footprints in the Crumps' front yard. There were rabbit and squirrel tracks, but no human ones. MP must not have come back in the middle of the night. I really wanted MP to return so we could spy.

"Where is Jay?" Kavita asked. "Shouldn't he be out here shoveling?"

I peered down the street at his house. "I don't see Meera Masi, Uncle Ryan, or Jay," I said. Meera Masi and Uncle Ryan are Jay's mom and dad.

Kavita rested her hands on her shovel. "Do you know what I think?" Before I could reply, she continued. "Jay and his parents must be sleeping. We should wake them up so they can get their driveway cleared."

Kavita started walking toward Jay's house. I didn't think waking them was a good idea. "Wait," I said and followed her. Then I realized something. "Look, Kavita. Jay's driveway is clean."

She stood on her tiptoes to see over the banks of snow. "That means they must have gotten up way earlier than us."

"Remember, Jay said he was going skiing with Jeff and Nora? They're probably on their way to the ski slope."

"Or they are already skiing," Kavita said.

I nodded. Jay's fun weekend had already started while I had to clear the snow and wait for our guests. And now I was worried. If our visitors didn't make it our fun weekend might not happen at all.

✳✳✳

After the snow-shovel exercise, Kavita and I had hot cocoa and Mom and Dad had their second cup of chai. We all deserved the special drinks.

De-serve means you work hard and can treat yourself to something special.

Dad's phone rang. He answered it on the first ring. It was Sanjay Uncle. He and Rita Auntie are not our real uncle and auntie, but that's what we call all our parents' Indian friends, and even some non-Indian ones. That's just how it is. Even though Priya and Nayan are not our cousins, calling their parents Uncle and Auntie kind of makes them feel like it.

Anyway, I knew the phone call was from Sanjay Uncle because Dad asked in Hindi, "Abhi tak nikle nahi?" It means "You haven't left yet?"

I was also surprised that they hadn't left yet. I worried that maybe they had canceled their trip. I tried to listen to their conversation. I couldn't hear Sanjay Uncle, but I could hear Dad perfectly well.

When Dad speaks Hindi with other people, I usually get the idea of what he is talking about. The problem is, I don't understand every single word. So I sometimes miss something important or get confused.

I listened carefully now. Dad advised Sanjay Uncle about how to drive in winter weather. Especially when there is snow.

"They're coming!" I whispered to Kavita.

"Are you sure?"

"Yes." I mean, why would Dad go on and on about icy bridges and snowdrifts if they weren't coming?

But then my head came up with a worry list.

* We already had snow, and Sanjay Uncle probably knew it would be hard to drive in it.

* They had recently moved from Florida, so they may have never driven in the snow.

* Dad's advice might make them nervous or even scare them.

* They might just decide to cancel the trip.

* Then we wouldn't have a special Snow Spy weekend with Priya and Nayan.

I had to stop Dad from scaring them. But how? It would be rude to talk to Dad while he was on the phone. I waved my arms. Dad put up his hand and mouthed, "Five more minutes."

I put a finger on my lips.

It worked!

Suddenly he went quiet. He was listening, but I couldn't hear Sanjay Uncle. I watched Dad's face to see if I could figure out what was going on.

Then Dad laughed. "Mai bhool gaya. I remember now. Chalo, milte hai. Still, be careful. Bye."

"Mai bhool gaya" means "I forgot." Then Dad said, "Chalo, milte hai," which means "Okay, see you," and hung up. It confused me. "What did you forget?" I asked Dad.

"I forgot that Sanjay and Rita used to live in Minneapolis. They know how to drive in wintry conditions."

"So, they didn't need your advice?"

"Advice?" Dad frowned. "I wasn't giving any advice."

"Oh yes you were," Mom said.

"Kavita, what do you think?" he asked.

"Dad, you're wise and full of advice. So, you give some. It's OK." She took the last sip of her hot cocoa. "But don't give away too much. If you do, you won't have any advice left."

"Thank you," Dad said and handed her a napkin. "You may want to wipe your mouth."

"See, that's advice," I pointed out.

"It was just a suggestion," he said.

Mom shook her head, I smiled, and Kavita took Dad's advice and wiped her mouth.

"I think they should be here by lunchtime," Mom said as she got up from the chair.

Dad took the teacups to the sink. "I can make all the beds."

I picked up my empty mug. "I will help."

"Don't forget me, the best helper around," Kavita said.

"Ha!" The word somersaulted out of my mouth as I remembered how Kavita had whined when Mom asked her to clean her room yesterday.

Good thing no one heard me, though.

"Nina, you help in the kitchen. Kavita, you help make beds. How does that sound?"

"Perfect, Mom," I said. When I cleaned up my room yesterday, I had made my bed. This morning I realized that I had to make my bed again. But I hadn't done it yet. Now Kavita and Dad were in charge of sleeping arrangements. That meant they would make beds and I didn't have to do it. Lucky!

"What are we making for lunch?" I asked Mom after Dad and Kavita went upstairs.

"How about spinach-cheese-rice?"

"I love that. Could we add garbanzo beans too?"

"Sure," Mom said. "Can you please get three cups of rice ready?"

I scooped out some rice with a measuring cup and put it into the rice cooker. I added water and sloshed the rice around before straining it. Then I added more water and sloshed again. "Do you think Sanjay Uncle and Rita Auntie will like this dish? It's not Indian food."

"Sanjay and Rita love it. We used to make it all the time when they lived in Minneapolis. Besides, Rita is from the Philippines."

"I didn't know that. Were they your best friends?"

"We're close friends."

"As close as you and Meera Masi?" I always thought Jay's mom was Mom's best friend.

"Nina, they all are my close friends. Meera Masi and I see each other almost every day now. You and Jay are the same age, and we are neighbors, so Meera Masi and I have a lot in common. But I have known Sanjay and Rita for many years. We have a lot of memories together. That is why I know they will enjoy what we're making for lunch. I hope Priya and Nayan like it too."

"I think they will. I wonder if they will become Kavita's and my friends."

"Of course, they will. Are you nervous?"

I shrugged. "Not really."

But I was a little worried. Since I was still washing rice, I couldn't write anything in Sakhi. So I made an in-my-head list.

* Sometimes friendships are hard to figure out.
* Jay was my friend. He was also friends with his cousins.
* I know his cousin Jeff a little, but we're not really friends.
* I don't know his cousin Nora at all.
* Would I ever become real friends with Jeff and Nora?
* Could Priya become friends with Jay?
* Or maybe Jay and Priya would be like Jay and Megan. They know each other but they're not really friends.
* Or they could become close friends. It was hard to tell.
* If we all become friends, would we forget how it all started?

* What if Jay and Priya become best friends?

* But Jay and I have been best friends for a long time.

* Maybe I shouldn't worry about Jay and me.

* Maybe I should work on being a better friend to him.

* And maybe that means trying to be less jealous of his time with other people.

* Maybe it would help if I made new friends this weekend and had my own time with other people.

Even though I had made a list about friendship, it was still a big, tangled web. Maybe I needed some help from Mom to figure this out. It felt kind of like solving a mystery. Like a spy does!

As soon as I thought about spying, I remembered MP. I looked out the window toward the Crumps' house. Everything looked peaceful and quiet.

While talking to Mom, I think I rinsed the rice three more times. It was enough. I had no time to dillydally anymore. I added water to the rice for cooking.

Dil-ly-dal-ly means when you waste time and don't finish the thing you are supposed to be doing.

Mom plugged in the rice cooker, and I opened the garbanzo bean cans. I rinsed the beans while Mom chopped onions.

I watched as she cooked onions, spinach, and beans in oil.

"What about cheese?" I asked.

"I'll shred the cheese, but we will wait until later to melt it and mix it with everything. That way it will stay warm and not turn rubbery. With this weather, I don't know when they will get in."

"Do you think they might not come?"

Mom took out a block of cheddar cheese. She cut me a piece before she started grating it. "They are on their way, but it might take them longer than it would without the snow."

Kavita and Dad came into the kitchen. "The beds are ready, and we have towels out for everyone," Dad said.

"Mom, I gave Priya a pink towel and Nayan a yellow one," Kavita said.

"That's very nice of you," Mom replied.

"You know why?" Kavita asked, then answered her own question. "Those're my favorite colors."

"I thought they were pink and green." I took a bite of my cheese.

Kavita took a small bowl to Mom. "I always like pink. But I like green in summer and yellow in winter."

Mom placed some shredded cheese in Kavita's bowl.

"Thanks, Mom." Kavita put some cheese in her mouth. "Sanjay Uncle and Rita Auntie are going to sleep in the guest room in the basement. Priya and Nayan are going to use my room. Can I stay with you, Nina?"

Sometimes my sister is so sweet, and I know we will always be friends. I smiled. "That would be great."

Everything was ready. All we needed was our guests. Then we could build our snow fort and be ready for spying. And we really needed MP to show up again!

CHAPTER FOUR

Finally, at 11:30, our guests arrived. They took off their jackets and Dad hung them up. I saw that Priya and Nayan had the right kind of boots to play outside. That made me happy. Sanjay Uncle and Rita Auntie hugged Mom and Dad. Priya, Nayan, Kavita, and I didn't do any hugging. Then we all went into the living room.

"You're so tall, Nina," Rita Auntie said to me as she took off her scarf. Mom extended her hand and took it and put it with their coats.

"Thanks." I don't know why, but I felt a little shy.

Rita Auntie turned to Kavita. "The last time I saw you, you were a baby. How old are you?"

"I'm six. It's grand to be in first grade," Kavita said.

"I'm sure it is."

"I am almost six," Nayan said.

"Looks like you enjoy being almost six," Dad said.

Nayan gave a missing-tooth smile.

"How are you, Priya?" Mom asked.

"Very well. Thank you," she replied.

I wondered if Priya was feeling shy too. Priya and Nayan both had brown eyes the color of a cinnamon stick. Priya was my height, but Nayan was shorter than Kavita.

Everyone else stayed in the living room, but I started setting the table in the dining room.

Priya came in. "What can I do to help?"

"Do you want to fill the water glasses?"

"Sure."

"Thanks!" I pointed to a cupboard. "They are in there."

When we sat down to eat, Nayan finished the food on his plate and asked, "Could I have a little more, Auntie?"

Mom served him again.

"You like spinach-cheese-rice as much as I do," Kavita said. "And you weren't even born in Wisconsin."

Nayan looked confused. "I don't understand."

"In Wisconsin we are cheeseheads, so we love cheese. I guess now you're one too."

Everyone laughed.

After we finished eating, Priya and I went to my room and Nayan went with Kavita. I introduced Priya to my stuffed beaver, Lucky. "Want to hold him?"

"Sure." Priya sat on my bed. "He is so soft and cuddly."

"Thanks, I bought him with my own money." I sat down next to her.

"That means Lucky is all yours."

"Yes, but I share him with my sister. I let her hold him, but he stays with me."

"That makes sense." Priya looked around the room. Then she pointed at Sakhi. "Do you keep a diary?"

"It's a notebook where I write my thoughts and lists."

"You make lists?"

"To stay organized." I didn't tell her about all the tracks running in my head.

"So do I." Priya put one finger up. "I make one list per day. At night I write down everything I'm planning to do the next day. I guess you make more than one?"

"Many more." What if Priya expected me to share Sakhi with her? But she didn't ask, and that made me like her even more.

Priya handed me Lucky. "What do you think Nayan and Kavita are doing?"

I heard footsteps. "They are in the hallway. I wonder if they're spying on us," I whispered. "Let's not say anything, because spies don't like to be caught."

"You're right," she mouthed the words.

I wondered if Mystery Person had noticed our spying. I knew MP couldn't have, though. We didn't have our snow fort set up or our spy team in action yet. All MP would have seen was Kavita and me rolling some snowballs.

I glanced out of the window at the Crumps' house.

Priya walked to the window. "What are you looking at, Nina?"

"Umm, nothing."

"You can really see your neighbors' house from here. Their roof is covered with snow!" Priya said. "There's so much snow everywhere!"

"Do you like snow?"

"Yes. Everything looks so beautiful after a snowfall," she said.

"Do you like Wisconsin or Florida better?" I asked her.

She looked thoughtful. "I've only been here for a short time, so I don't know which place I like better yet."

"I have never lived anywhere else," I said. "In Wisconsin we have four different seasons, and you can do something special in each one. In spring it is wonderful to see grass turn green and flowers pop out of the ground, in summer it is such a treat to go to farmers' markets for fresh fruits and vegetables, and in fall all the trees are so colorful that you feel like you're in a painting."

"What about winter?"

"I love playing in snow," I said. "I love building things, like snowmen and snow forts."

Kavita peeked out from behind the door. "Priya, don't you love building a snowman?"

"I've never built one. I've only lived in Florida, and it doesn't snow there," Priya said.

Kavita looked shocked. "You have never ever seen snow before?"

"Not until a few weeks ago."

Nayan walked into my room. "Can we make a snowman? Right now?"

I put Lucky on the bed and stood up. "Let's do it."

Downstairs, our parents were gathered around the fireplace talking. "Is it OK if we play in the snow, Mom?" I asked.

She glanced at Priya's mom.

"Isn't it too cold to go out?" Rita Auntie asked.

"Not for making a snowman!" Nayan said.

"You're right, Nayan. It's a perfect day to make a snow-man," Mom said. She asked, "Rita, have you forgotten Minneapolis? If they wear hats, mittens, and jackets, they should be fine, right?"

"Kavita and I have extra pairs of socks. We will all put on two pairs so our feet stay warm," I said.

"OK," Rita Auntie replied, but she sounded doubtful. She added, "Also, put a sweater on."

Doubt-ful means feeling not sure because you're full of doubt.

"And if you get cold, come in the house," Mom said.

Kavita and I like the cold. If we get chilly, we go inside to warm up. Mom knows that. I think she was worried about Priya and Nayan. "We will."

I guess if you come from Florida, the Wisconsin winter might seem too cold. Maybe Rita Auntie was worried that Nayan and Priya wouldn't enjoy it at all. Today the sun shone brightly, though, and the temperature was in the twenties. It was a perfect snow-playing day.

We bundled up and headed out. I scanned the street for Jay. I wished Jay, Jeff, and Nora were playing in the snow. Of course, I didn't see them. They were having fun skiing. Still, I had my own team. We were going to build our snow fort. Then we were going to spy!

That's why I wasn't disappointed about not having Jay to play with too.

> **Dis-ap-point** means when something doesn't work out so you feel kind of sad.

"Time to build a snow fort," I said.

"Not a snow fort," Nayan said. "A snowman!"

I had forgotten about promising to build the snowman. I must have looked surprised, because Priya said, "A snow fort sounds like a fun thing to build, Nayan."

He pouted. "Not as much fun as a snowman."

I made a quick in-my-head list.

- ✻ I had agreed to build a snowman.

- ✻ Nayan was excited about it.

- ✻ Like Priya, this was his first-ever snowman.

- ✻ Nayan and Priya were our guests.

- ✻ Nayan was much younger than me.

- ✻ Priya and Nayan were not used to staying out in the cold and might want to go back in the house before long.

- ✻ That's why we should make a snowman first.

- ✻ There was no one around, so our spying could wait.

"Nayan, just because you're the youngest, you don't always get what you want," Priya said. "Nina wants to build a fort."

"Let's make the snowman first." I looked at Kavita. "Is that OK?"

"Yay!"

"Nayan, once the snowman is done, we will build a snow fort," Priya said. "Agree?"

"Opo."

Kavita put her hands on her hips. "Why are you saying 'Opo'?"

Nayan's eyes danced. "It means 'yes.'"

"'Opo' doesn't mean 'yes.' Only 'yes' means 'yes,'" Kavita said.

Priya explained. "'Opo' means 'yes' in Tagalog."

"Oh!" Kavita was silent for a moment. "Just like 'haan' means 'yes' in Hindi?"

"Yes," Nayan said.

"Opo," Kavita repeated. She sang, *"Opo means yes, like haan means yes. Opo and haan mean yes and yes."*

"That's right!" Nayan pointed at the snow pile by our driveway. "How do you make a snowman?"

Kavita kneeled by the pile. "I'll show you." She began rolling the snow.

Nayan did the same.

"Want to help me make a bigger ball right here?" I asked Priya.

"Why bigger?"

They really had no experience in making a snowman. None whatsoever. "For the base."

Priya and I made a huge snowball. I took a few steps backward to examine it. It needed a little rounding out. I slapped on more snow until it was perfectly round. Now came the challenging part. "We have to get Kavita's and Nayan's snowball on top of ours without dropping it," I said.

Nayan sprang up. "I'll carry it." But when he tried to lift it up, he couldn't even move it.

"I think we need more than one person. How about Priya and I do that while you and Kavita make the snowman's head?"

"Opo," Kavita said.

Nayan clapped. "You're talking in Tagalog!"

"Let's go over to where there is fresh snow." Kavita

sang, *"Fresh snow, best snow. Head snow, tail snow,"* as she and Nayan walked away.

Why couldn't Kavita suppress her song making and singing for a couple of days?

> **Sup-press** means to not let anyone know about something by keeping it to yourself.

Priya glanced at Kavita. "That's the second time she's sung." She smiled at me. "It's so sweet."

I wondered if Priya would still find it sweet if she had to listen to Kavita's songs every single day. Ten times a day. I stayed quiet.

Priya and I lifted the ball together. It was heavy and we could barely raise it high enough to put it on the top of the base.

"Oh no," she said. "Part of it broke."

"That's an easy fix." I stuck some more snow on it and made sure the middle part of the snowman wasn't lopsided.

"Head, head, we'll make a head. Big and round and jolly one too," Kavita sang.

"Why does Kavita sing so much?" Priya whispered.

I realized something.

> In-my-head list about Kavita's singing
>
> ✱ Kavita is my sister, so I know her well.
>
> ✱ This was Priya's first time meeting her.
>
> ✱ Priya probably had no idea before arriving that Kavita sings.
>
> ✱ Now they know because Kavita had already done it three times.
>
> ✱ Priya and Nayan probably don't sing made-up song anytime, anywhere like Kavita does. And probably their friends don't either.
>
> ✱ Priya must think all of this is strange.
>
> ✱ I couldn't let Priya think my sister is weird.

"Kavita is very creative," I said. "That is why she makes up songs. It helps her think better. Isn't that a super-smart thing to do?" I hoped I had convinced Priya that Kavita is super-smart.

"Does she sing about different things?"

"Oh yes," I replied. "Kavita sings about snow and seasons, flowers and gardens, paintings, and even about her room."

Priya laughed. "Kavita's snow songs are fun. Are they all like that?"

"Most of the time."

Priya looked at Kavita like she really thought Kavita was someone special. My sister certainly was.

Kavita and Nayan carried the snowman's head together. But when they tried to put it on the very top, they couldn't reach to do it. The head slipped and hit the snowy ground.

It crashed without a sound and fell apart.

"The head broke!" Nayan looked upset, ready to cry.

"It wasn't the head," Kavita said. "It was just a big snowball. I can fix it." She leaned over and started packing the head back together.

"No! It was my snowman's head." Tears rolled down his cheeks. He trudged through the snow toward the house.

"Come back," Priya said.

Nayan stopped, but he didn't turn around. "How can we have a snowman without a head?"

"It is fixed!" Kavita shouted. She was already done.

Nayan returned. As soon as he saw it, he jumped, then flopped onto the snow. "You fixed it so fast, Kavita!"

"Yup. I'm a magician."

He got up. "No, you're not."

"I can fix this, I can fix that. I can make that snowman again. I can sing, I can dance, because I am a magician!"

Nayan giggled.

No more Kavita and Nayan arguing. Phew!

Now I could find the perfect place to build our snow fort.

My eyes rested on a spot a few feet behind the clump of spruce trees. They would give us added protection from the wind. It was on a slight slope, so we wouldn't have to make our snow fort very tall. We would be up high enough that people couldn't see us. Spies never announce their mission to the whole world.

"Nina, Nina," Priya called.

When I started thinking about the snow fort, I forgot about the headless snowman. My old thoughts do go missing lots of times when new ones arrive.

"Coming," I said.

"Kavita and Nayan can't reach the top. Can you help me place the head?" Priya asked.

I glanced around and panicked. "Where are they?"

Priya pointed at the house. "Kavita said she needed some things for the snowman."

"Stuff to make its nose, eyes, and mouth," I said.

"Oh."

Priya and I carefully picked up the snowball and placed it on the top of the two rounds.

I heard a car drive down our street. I whirled around to see the mail truck.

"The carrier didn't stop at the Crumps' house," I said.

Priya shrugged. "Maybe they didn't have any mail."

In-my-head list of why the mail carrier didn't stop at the Crumps' house and what I should do about it

* Like Priya said, maybe there was no mail for the Crumps today.

* Like Dad said, maybe the Crumps had stopped the mail delivery.

* I would find out Monday if the mail had been delivered to them that day.

* Monday was just a school holiday, so the mail would still come.

* Then I could see if MP showed up again.

* If MP showed up, I could check the Crumps' mailbox after MP left to see if their mail was gone.

* Would I get in trouble for snooping in their mailbox?

I was still thinking about my options when Priya asked, "Are there kids in that house?"

"No. Mr. and Mrs. Crump are retired and they're in Arizona."

"Are you keeping an eye on their house while they're away?"

"Why do you ask?"

"Because," Priya said, "you kept looking at their house from your room, and you glanced again when we came out, and you checked just now when the mail carrier came."

Priya was a good spy without even trying to be one. Remarkable!

Re-mark-a-ble means something special that you notice.

"You're right." I lowered my voice. "I am watching their house. Yesterday, Kavita and I saw a stranger taking something from their mailbox. That mystery person might return today."

Her eyes widened in surprise. "A man or a woman?"

"I'm not sure. That's why we call the suspect Mystery Person, MP for short. If we build a snow fort, we can spy on MP from inside it."

Priya rubbed her mittened hands. "This is so exciting."

Kavita and Nayan returned with a carrot, two black olives, and a slice of red apple. Nayan stood on his tiptoes and stuck the olives in the snowman's face.

"They're too low," Kavita said. "It makes our snowman's head look huge."

"You don't like it?" Nayan asked.

"Nope." She sang, *"A huge-headed snowman is not what I want. A huge-headed snowman is not what I build."*

"Then you move them up," Nayan said. "I can't reach any higher."

Kavita moved the olives—I mean the eyes—up. Once the mouth and nose also found their proper places, the snowman was ready. But not quite. *Should I say anything or just stay quiet?* I wondered.

Mom called out, "Come and get it."

I ran to her. She handed me an old scarf and a hat. "Thanks, Mom. How did you know I wanted these?"

"Because I'm your mom."

That made me snow-sparkling happy.

I tied the scarf around the snowman's neck (which is really where the two top rounds meet). Priya put the hat on the snowman's head.

"It's done!" Kavita clapped and jumped. It is hard to jump in deep snow, but she did try.

So did Nayan. "The best snowman I ever built!"

"It's the first snowman you ever built. But you didn't build it all by yourself," Kavita said. "We all did. It belongs to all of us."

"It was my idea," Nayan said.

"It is in Kavita's and Nina's yard, so it belongs to them too," Priya said.

Nayan looked sad. "We won't be able to take him with us, Priya."

"That's right. He will stay here."

"OK," he said. "Our best snowman ever. Is it OK if I name it?"

I didn't care if he named it, but I wanted to make sure it was OK with Kavita. "How about you give him the first name and Kavita can give him the last name?"

"Snowy," Nayan said.

"Soni," Kavita said.

"Snowy Soni sounds syrupy sweet," I whispered to Priya.

"They like it." She glanced at Nayan and Kavita, who were rolling more snow. "Maybe they are making an entire Snowy Soni family."

"Don't give them that idea," I said. "We can use their snowballs for our snow fort. It will be our spy base."

CHAPTER FIVE

Priya glanced around the yard. "What's the best spot for our snow fort?"

"I have a place in mind," I said. "Right behind that clump of spruce trees."

We began making the snow fort by rolling big snowballs. "Let's make a row of ten," I said. "That way it will be easy to count how many we have."

"Great idea."

We had four rows.

10 snowballs x 4 rows = 40 snowballs

We arranged them in a semicircle behind the trees.

I backed up and examined our work.

Ex-am-ine means to really look closely at something to make sure it is done well.

"Don't you think it looks good?"

"Perfect!" Priya replied.

"We need a lot more snowballs for the wall," I said.

Kavita asked, "Can Nayan and I make them for you?"

Nayan scooped up snow. "It's the most fun."

Priya and I exchanged a knowing glance. How lucky we were!

"Yes!" I said. "Thank you."

"'I don't really know how to make walls," Priya said to me. "How about if I bring the snowballs to you?"

I didn't want Priya to feel like she had the least important job and I had the most important one. "It's more fun to build it together."

"OK. I'll try."

We kneeled again. "I think this is more difficult than building a sandcastle," Priya said.

"Did you live on a beach in Florida?" I asked.

She placed a snowball on top of the bottom layer of the wall. "No, but close to it. We went there a lot."

I sculpted the snowballs into another layer of wall. "The good thing about wet snow is that you can connect and shape it easily. Dry snow is difficult to work with."

"It's almost like wet or dry sand," Priya said.

We had been working for a while when a gust of wind came. Priya shivered.

"Are you cold?" I asked.

"A little."

I pointed at her face. "Your cheeks are red. Should we take a break?"

"Yes." She called out, "Nayan and Kavita, let's go into the house to warm up."

Nayan didn't move. "No!"

Kavita whispered something in his ear.

"Opo!" he said, then got up and dashed toward the house.

Priya looked surprised. "What did Kavita tell him?"

"When we go in from playing in the snow, we get to drink hot cocoa. I think that's what she must have told Nayan."

"No wonder he changed his mind." Then she asked, "How will we keep an eye on the Crumps' house if we're inside?"

Like me, Priya was serious about spying. I liked that.

"Come." I held my hand out. "As long as we sit at the kitchen counter, we can still see."

We followed Kavita and Nayan into the house. Mom had put an old rug in the mudroom.

"Nayan, you have to take everything off here, before we enter the kitchen," Kavita said.

"Why?"

"That's the hot cocoa rule."

We all took off our mittens, shoes, socks, scarves, and jackets. Nayan began to take off his shirt.

"You keep that on," I said quickly. Just to make sure, I added, "And your pants."

"Kavita said I have to take everything off if I—"

"Even with your shirt on, you'll get hot cocoa," I assured him.

Kavita held his hand. "Come with me."

"Kavita really knows how to make him cooperate," Priya whispered. "I wonder who she learned it from?"

I shrugged. "Not from me." Then I thought about how I usually get Kavita to do what I want her to do.

Priya's eyes twinkled, as if she could read my mind.

It was nice to make a new friend. Especially this weekend while Jay was busy with Jeff and Nora.

Priya and I carried everything downstairs. I threw our cold and kind of wet socks, mittens, and coats in the dryer and lined up our boots by the heat registers before we went back upstairs.

We sat at the kitchen counter with hot cocoa and mini marshmallows in each of our mugs.

"Be careful. It's hot," I warned everyone.

I took a deep breath, and the chocolaty smell made me want to take a sip right away. But I had to wait. If I didn't, then I would burn my tongue, and it would feel all bumpy and grumpy for a long time.

Priya and I watched the Crumps' house between sips. It was fun that she was as interested in being a spy as I was. After warming up, we went down to get our jackets and boots.

Priya said, "I didn't see anyone at the Crumps' house. Did you?"

I opened the dryer. "No. Too bad MP has not returned."

"Who is MP?" Nayan asked.

Priya brought everyone's boots. "It's a mystery person. That's why we say MP. We don't know who it is."

Nayan sat down. "Why are we talking about someone we don't know?"

Kavita handed Nayan his socks. "MP was here yesterday, so we kind of know MP."

"OK." Nayan pulled up his socks. He wiggled his toes. "I love toasted socks."

"Not as much as hot cocoa with marshmallows, though, right?" Kavita asked.

"Good one," Priya said as we went upstairs.

∗∗∗

Our semicircle fort was about three feet tall. As I sculpted the wall, I made four little shelves, one for each of us. Then I thought of Jay. What if he came over to play? What if Jeff and Nora came too? There wasn't enough space to make three more shelves. I guessed we could share. I also didn't fill in the snow between each and every snowball. We could use that space as spy holes.

Priya brought in more snowballs. She watched me for a while. "Should we fill in the spaces between all of them?"

"I left some of them open on purpose. They're spy holes," I said. "Do you like them? The top ones are for us, and the lower ones are for Kavita and Nayan."

"I love that we have spy holes!" She kneeled and looked through one of the lower ones. "I can see the house across the street. But I don't think anyone there could see me."

"Let's check to make sure."

I crossed the street and walked toward Jay's house. I stood in front of it. I could hardly see the fort. I certainly couldn't see Priya. I went up and down the street to make sure our fort was well hidden. Finally I stopped in the Crumps' driveway. I could see a little part of the fort, but most of it was hidden. Yay for evergreen spruce trees!

When I came back, Priya asked, "Could you see me?"

"Not at all. I could barely even see the fort."

Nayan and Kavita were still making snowballs. Suddenly Kavita busted out singing. *"Spruce, spruce, you are not Bruce. Still, you're my friend, spruce."*

I sighed. "Sometimes Kavita's singing can get too much and too loud."

Priya nodded. "I can see that. Has she always sung so much?"

Kavita's singing probably felt really strange to Priya, and she was curious about it. Or by now she was also getting tired of all of Kavita's made-up songs. I said, "Kavita loves singing. As far back as I can remember. I guess not before she could talk, but I don't remember that time."

Kavita and Nayan came over. Kavita tugged my arm. "We're done rolling snowballs. I want to tumblogan!"

"Tumblogan?" Nayan asked.

"How do you do that?" Priya looked confused.

Priya and Nayan didn't realize that Kavita had mispronounced "toboggan."

Mis-pro-nounce means you don't say a word correctly.

"To-bog-gan," I said slowly. "You sit on a toboggan and slide down a snowy hill. We have to go to Cherokee School for that. It's only a ten-minute drive."

"Tobogganing is so much fun! Don't forget to take a turn.

Down, down, down. Crash and tumble. Climb back up to slide right down," Kavita sang. This time she said it right.

"I don't want to go down a big slope." Nayan looked worried. "What about the fort? Can't we play in it?"

I think Kavita had scared him with "crash and tumble."

"Sure."

All four of us crouched behind the fort wall. It was wide enough that we didn't have to huddle, and we each had our own spy hole.

"What are the shelves for?" Kavita asked.

"To put our spy equipment on."

E-quip-ment means things you need in order to do something, like a pair of binoculars or a notebook to write down what you see when you're spying.

Then I realized that the binoculars would get ruined in the snow, and a notebook would get wet. The shelves would only be good for keeping things cold. "Or for snacks," I said.

Kavita fingered her shelf. "Hey, we could get popsicles and store them here."

"Great idea," I agreed.

Priya shoved her hands in her jacket pockets. "I don't want a popsicle in this freezing weather."

Nayan said, "This is boring."

Priya was freezing, Nayan was bored, and a popsicle was not an option.

We needed some excitement. We didn't have anyone to spy on. Most of our neighbors had shoveled their snow and gone back inside. Now our street was quiet and empty. And boring. If only MP would show up so we could spy!

But for that to be a possibility, we had to stay outside and wait.

"Do you want to make snow angels?" I asked.

"Yes!" Nayan shouted. Then asked, "How do you do that?"

The snow in our front yard was all trampled up and scooped up. For fresh snow, we had to go into the backyard, which is also a side yard on the other street. And it is not fenced in. That's why I couldn't let Kavita and Nayan go alone. I had to be with them to make sure they were safe.

"Your backyard is like a giant snow mattress," Priya said.

She was right. It really looked like that. "We're going to lie down on that mattress," I said.

"I'll show you what to do." Kavita laid on her back and began moving her arms and feet in the snow. Then she got up. "Look!" Kavita pointed at her creation. "Isn't that the most perfect snow angel you ever saw?"

"It's a very beautiful snow angel," Priya said.

Kavita tugged at her sleeve. "Let's make more."

Soon our snow mattress was covered with snow angels.

Then Mom called. "You have been out too long. Time to come in."

"Do we get hot cocoa again?" Nayan asked.

"No," I said.

"But we're coming in from the cold."

"Hot cocoa once a day. No way, twice a day," Kavita sang.

Even though today Kavita and I had already had hot cocoa after shoveling the snow, I didn't mention it.

"Why do you make up songs for everything, Kavita?" Nayan asked.

"Because they are fun, and I love them."

"More than snow angels, hot cocoa, and snowmen?" he asked.

"Yes. Songs are always there when I need them."

I guess Kavita's song making is like my list making. They're essential.

Es-sen-tial means something you really need.

"Are you coming in?" Mom called again.

Priya and I glanced at the Crumps' house before going in.

Would MP ever return?

CHAPTER SIX

That evening we went to Paisan's for pizza. Meera Masi joined us.

"I wish Jay and Uncle Ryan could have come too," I said to Meera Masi when we walked inside the restaurant.

"Me too. But they won't be back from skiing until later in the evening."

We were seated at a long table. Priya was next to me. She whispered, "Who are Jay and Uncle Ryan?"

The waiter handed me a menu as I answered. "Jay is Meera Masi's and Uncle Ryan's son. He is our age."

"Do you think we will see him tomorrow?"

"I hope we see Jay and his cousins Jeff and Nora." I explained, "They're spending a couple of days with him."

Then we both read the menu.

All the adults had pizza with hot banana peppers and spicy cheese. The kids had veggie pizza without any hot peppers.

When we got home from dinner, I asked my parents, "Can we stay outside just for a little while?"

"No, it's late," Dad replied.

"We went to dinner super-early. It is not even seven."

"True," Mom said. "It's dark, though. I don't want you to be out alone."

"Sanjay and I will walk Meera to her house. We can stay out for a while so you can play in your fort," Dad said.

Sanjay Uncle laughed. "Brrrrr."

They crossed the street and walked on the opposite side. They waited until Meera Masi got into her house before turning around. Our street is only a block long, so Dad and Sanjay Uncle could never be too far away. Now we could spy safely.

"Did you see that the Crumps' driveway is clean?" I asked.

"MP must have shoveled it," Kavita said.

"Why do you talk about MP so much?" Nayan wanted to know.

"Because MP might be stealing from our neighbors," I explained.

"Stealing snow?" Nayan put his hand on his mouth as if snow was the most precious thing.

"Maybe MP wants to build a giant snowman? Much bigger than ours," Kavita said.

"I don't think so." Priya shook her head. "Nina, MP must have been here while we were away for dinner."

We looked for signs of MP but there weren't any: no car, no lights, no open garage.

"Let's watch and see," I said.

We ducked behind the snow fort.

Then we waited.

And waited some more.

Nayan tapped my shoulder. "We built this fort to spy, but there is no one to spy on."

"It's OK." Kavita sang, *"Spy on sky, spy on pie. Spy, spy, spy until you fly, fly, fly."*

Nayan laughed. "Your song is silly."

"I love silly songs. They're the best kind to make up and sing."

"You're a great song-maker and singer, Kavita," Priya said.

In the shimmer of streetlight and snow I could see Kavita's beaming smile. "I'm a *grand* song-maker."

"Doesn't look like MP is here." Priya looked at me. "Who should we spy on?"

It had been my idea to build a snow fort and to spy, so I guessed I was the leader. That meant it was my job to come up with something to do.

The street was peaceful and empty except for Dad and Sanjay Uncle walking back.

"Let's eavesdrop on our dads," I said. "It's almost like spying and it will be fun, right?"

We waited for them to come to the front of the house. They walked past us and kept on going to the end of the sidewalk. But we couldn't hear a word they said.

Nayan got up. "This is boring."

"Almost-spying is boring, just like snoring," Kavita sang. "Let's go inside and draw some spies."

"Opo," Nayan said.

Hand in hand, they left.

I sighed.

"I wish Jay and his cousins were here. Then we could spy on them," Priya said.

Spy on Jay? I was baffled.

Baf-fled means you don't know how to feel or what to do about something.

Sure, I wanted to spy. But on Jay? Kavita had said it is not nice to spy on friends and neighbors. But Kavita,

Nayan, Priya, and I had almost-spied on our dads. Not that we could find out anything. Why didn't I feel right about spying on Jay then?

I made an in-my-head list of why it didn't feel right to spy on Jay.

* Usually a country spies on an enemy country to find out what they are doing. Jay is my best friend and he already tells me his plans.

* People spy on other people when they don't trust them or like them. I trust Jay and I like him.

* People who spy hide the fact that they are spying. I mean, no spy says, "Hey, I am spying on you" to the person they are spying on. They hide the truth. I don't know if I could hide the truth from Jay.

* I couldn't spy on him.

Priya had waited patiently for my answer.

"I really don't think I want to spy on Jay."

"Oh?" she said.

Dad called out. "Time to go in."

I was happy about that.

When we went inside the house, Kavita and Nayan were coloring superheroes but not spies. Priya and I played cards with our parents and kept an eye on the Crumps' house. No activity there.

✳✳✳

At night, Priya came into my room. "I wish I could sleep here so we can keep on spying."

I shook my head. "MP is not here, so how can we spy?"

"You're right." She picked up Lucky. "We could stay up and talk. Maybe MP might come back tonight."

"Nina, can I sleep in my room?" Kavita asked from the doorway. "Nayan wants to be with his parents."

"How would you like to have your room by yourself? Priya can stay with me."

"Yay!" Kavita sang, *"My room, my room, I have my very own room. Room to roam, room to zoom. Roam-zoom, roam-zoom!"*

"Yay for us too," Priya said.

By the time we brushed our teeth and changed into our pj's, Kavita and Nayan were probably asleep.

"Even though we don't have anyone to spy on, do you want to make a list of spy words?" I asked Priya.

"That sounds like fun."

I opened Sakhi and we made a list. I wrote a *P* next to the words Priya suggested.

Nina and Priya's Spy Words

* Spy
* Spymaster (P)
* Spy base
* Sleuth
* Undercover (P)
* Hide

* Code Name (P)

* Eavesdrop

* Information (P)

* Secret

* Signal (P)

I tapped my pen. "There have to be more words."

"'Espionage,'" Priya said.

I had never heard that word before. "What does it mean?"

"It means 'spying.' It comes from French."

Priya knew words that I did not. It made me feel a little lost for not knowing and a little excited for learning something new. "Thanks."

She spelled it and I added it to the list. "Any others?"

"I can't think of one." She shook her head. "I'm sure we're missing a ton of words."

"Probably. I wish I hadn't left my tablet downstairs. We

could have looked up all the spy words," I said. "Now if we go down to get it our parents will ask us to go to bed."

"And once they ask, we have to do it."

"Exactly," I said.

"Maybe we can get it without them knowing."

"It could be our mission. Operation Tablet Rescue," I said.

"Hey, that's three more spy words."

I added them. Then I wrote *N and P* next to them. I had said those words, and Priya had pointed out that they were spy words.

✳	Mission (N and P)
✳	Operation (N and P)
✳	Rescue (N and P)

We snuck downstairs. No lights. Had our parents gone to bed?

"Where is your tablet?" Priya whispered.

"In the family room." We crept closer.

As I opened the door, I heard voices and saw light spill out from the TV screen. Someone coughed. My tablet was trapped on a coffee table between the TV and the couch. There was no way we could get it out.

Time to retreat.

> **Re-treat** means go back to where you came from or give up on what you were doing.

The lights came on.

Four pairs of eyes fixed on us.

We froze.

"It's late. Why are you two still up?" Mom asked.

Priya and I looked at each other.

"We're thirsty," Priya said.

"The kitchen is on the opposite side of the family room." I could see Mom trying to hide her smile.

Priya and I got some water and went back to my room without my tablet.

Our mission Operation Tablet Rescue was unsuccessful.

I added one more word to the spy list.

✳ Unsuccessful

CHAPTER SEVEN

On Sunday morning Jay was in his driveway with Jeff and Nora. I wasn't in my fort, but I could see them from my bedroom window. Nora had a mug in her hand. I wondered if it was tea, coffee, or hot cocoa.

Nora pointed in our direction. Why was she doing that? Were they talking about me? Could she see our snow fort? Yesterday when I looked from Jay's yard, I couldn't see it because the spruces hid it.

"Let's change clothes and quickly go outside," I said to Priya.

When we went downstairs, Mom said, "Kavita and Nayan already ate breakfast. There's warm oatmeal on the table. I will cut apples for you."

"Can we eat later?" I asked.

Mom shook her head. "Breakfast first."

Priya and I scooped oatmeal into our bowls and added cinnamon and raisins. We gulped our breakfast down quickly. That is one good thing about oatmeal. It is faster and easier to eat than even cereal and milk. Especially if someone makes it for you!

Rita Auntie sat at the table. "Are you sure you two want to go out so early? Isn't it cold?"

"Not at all." Priya shoveled the last spoonful of her oatmeal into her mouth.

"You're getting used to Wisconsin weather very nicely, Priya," Mom said.

"It is even more fun to play in the snow than the sand," Priya said as we took our empty dishes to the sink.

Just like the day before, we got ready by putting on

two pairs of socks and tons of clothes. Mom handed us a bowl of apple slices to take outside.

Nayan didn't want to come out, and Kavita wanted to play with him, so she stayed inside too. I was surprised. Usually Kavita follows me.

In-my-head list of reasons Kavita didn't want to come with me

* Nayan is only here for one more day, so Kavita wants to spend time with him.

* He is younger than Kavita, which means she can boss him.

* Kavita doesn't want Priya and me telling her what to do.

* Kavita and Nayan enjoy being with each other.

* Even though Kavita is my sister, she needs a break from me.

Wait a minute, why would she need a break from me?

Then I realized I also enjoy time away from Kavita. It is great to have my own friend. And to not have to share that friend with anyone else.

Priya and I put the bowl of apple slices on one of our snow shelves. Sometimes after it snows, the weather turns very windy and bitter cold, but that didn't happen this time. It was a perfect day to be outdoors.

We made snowballs and watched the street. Jay, Jeff, and Nora had disappeared. Unlike our yard, Jay's yard had not been trampled over and looked fresh.

Priya and I crouched behind the snow fort, waiting for something to happen, for someone to drive by, for somebody to walk their dog. That way we could spy.

Then I heard Nora's squeal and Jay's laughter.

I looked through a spy hole. "That's Nora and Jay."

Priya tugged at my arm. "This is so exciting."

"Huh?"

"We can see them perfectly, but they can't see us. It's finally our chance to spy."

"But I already know pretty much everything about Jay." I munched on an apple slice. "We won't find anything new."

"Then we could almost-spy like we did on our dads," Priya said. "It'll be more fun than we had last night."

Before I could say anything, Jeff came out. He bent down and scooped up some snow.

"That must be Jeff," Priya said.

"Yes. Looks like he is getting ready for an attack on Jay and Nora."

Jeff threw a snowball and hit Jay.

"You're right," Priya said.

Jay chased Jeff. Nora took a sip from her mug before putting it down on the front stoop. She scooped up snow.

And then the snowball fight really started.

Priya took an apple slice. We both munched and watched them running, throwing, and squealing.

I was so engrossed that I forgot where I was or that Priya was with me.

> **En-grossed** means you're paying all your attention to one thing and you forget all the other things.

Just then Jay looked in our direction, but I didn't think he could see us.

"Do you know Jeff and Nora well?" Priya asked.

"I know Jeff a little, but not Nora."

"Your mom and Meera Masi are friends. Do you like Jay?"

I didn't know how to answer Priya. If I told her I like him Priya might think I like him like a girl likes a boy. But I couldn't say I don't like Jay because I do like him. It seemed better to just say the way it is. "I have known Jay all my life."

"You're lucky." She sighed. "It is so difficult to move. I had to leave all my friends when we came to Wisconsin. Now that I have met you, I hope you don't move away. We could be best friends, right?"

I wished I had already told Priya that Jay is my best friend. I wanted to be friends with Priya, but Jay is Jay. I can't replace him with anyone else.

"We're already friends, Priya."

She handed me an apple slice. "Yes, we are."

We looked over the top of our snow fort so we could see Jay's entire yard.

Jay flung a snowball at Jeff. It hit him on the arm, and he chased Jay. Nora was making a snowball fast and furiously.

"What did she do with her mug? She put it on the stoop, but it's not there anymore," I said.

"I don't know. When we started talking, we lost track of them," Priya said. "We're not good spies. We need more training. Hey, 'training,' that's one more word for our spy list."

"Sure."

Before Nora could throw her snowball, Jeff hit her with one. Then he chased Jay, who ran down the sidewalk.

He was so close! It was my perfect chance to hit him! I couldn't resist. I picked up a snowball, stood up, and stepped sideways to get out from behind the trees. I threw it with all my energy.

It missed the target and hit one of the mailboxes. I ducked back down.

"Ha! Jeff, don't snowball the mailbox," Jay said.

"I didn't." Jeff opened his hand. "I still have mine."

Jeff and Jay came closer to the mailbox to scrutinize the scene of the crime.

Scru-ti-nize means to study something very closely.

"Now, Priya," I whispered.

Priya laughed quietly. Our eyes met and without saying a word we each picked up a snowball. We stepped out from behind the trees and aimed at Jeff and Jay, hitting them both at the same time. We hid behind the fort.

Jeff searched. "No one's here."

"I thought I saw someone move," Jay said.

"Must be the branches."

They came closer. They didn't see our fort behind the tree, or maybe they just pretended not to.

Priya and I stifled a giggle.

"No one is here," Jeff said again and walked away.

We stepped out. This time our snowballs landed next to them.

They whipped around.

We crouched down behind the trees and crawled back into the fort.

"There were two snowballs," Jeff said. "At the same time!"

"Yup. I saw them," Jay said. "It might be Nina, but Kavita is too young to throw a snowball this far. It must be someone else."

Jeff moved closer to the driveway. "Who could it be?"

Priya and I covered our mouths to muffle our laughter.

"Oh, I know! Nina said they had guests this weekend," Jay said. "I bet that's their car."

As soon as they walked up our driveway, Jay spotted the fort and pointed at it. "They're in there."

Priya peeked above it. "Are you talking to me?"

Without thinking about it, I stood up too.

Jay waved. "Nina!"

I waved back. "Come on over."

Jay did. "This is awesome, Nina! Did you make it?"

"Not alone. Kavita, Priya, Nayan, and I built it," I said. Then I introduced Priya to Jay and Jeff.

Priya was not anonymous to them anymore.

A-non-y-mous means someone who stays unknown.

She could still hide and spy on them but as soon as they found out she was spying, they would know who she was.

"Jay and Jeff, come on back!" Nora shouted from Jay's house.

Jay glanced back at her. "Coming." He turned to me. "Nina, do you guys want to come over?"

"Do you?" I asked Priya.

"Sure," she said. "Shouldn't we tell our parents?"

"If we do, Kavita will want to come with us."

"And then Nayan will too. Nayan is my brother, and he is five," Priya explained.

"They may not like a snowball fight," I said. "I don't want them to cry if a snowball hits them."

"Stop discussing, start walking," Jay said over his shoulder.

"Yes. In a minute." I turned to Priya. "We can call them from Jay's house. Take a couple of snowballs. You'll need them."

We crossed the street and followed Jay and Jeff. Our street is one of the last ones to get plowed because it's short, so it hadn't been cleared yet.

Before we got to Jay's house, a snowball hit me on the side. I threw one back quickly. Unfortunately, it banged into a bush.

"Get Jeff," I said to Priya. She aimed and hit him square in the face.

"There are two of you," Jeff groaned, wiping snow off his face. "Not fair."

"There are three of you," I shouted back. "Yes, it is not fair."

"But Nora and Jay just went in."

"Not our problem."

Jeff casually picked up some snow and rolled it into a ball. Priya and I noticed, and we quickly did the same. Now we stood face-to-face with him.

Jay came out of the garage with a toboggan.

Priya turned and looked. "Is that for sledding?"

Wham! A snowball hit her shoulder. She swirled around and ran after Jeff. Her snowball landed on his back.

I hit Jay with mine.

"I wasn't ready," he said.

"You asked us to come over. Anyway, a snowball fight doesn't have a start and a stop time," I said.

"Still, I have this in my hands." He put the toboggan down. "Time out." Jay signaled as if this was a football game.

"OK." We all stood around with empty hands.

"Is that some kind of sled?" Priya asked again.

"It's a toboggan. A snow slide, like I told you about. You sit on it and whoosh down the snowy slope. It's super-fun," I said.

"Jeff, Nora, and I are going tobogganing," Jay said. "My dad will drop us off. Do you want to come?"

I was happy he had asked me to go with them but I didn't want to ditch Priya. He must have read the concern on my face because Jay added, "I already talked to my parents. They told me to ask Priya too."

I made an in-my-head list.

* I wanted to go with Jay. And he had invited Priya too.

* That way I would get to know Jeff and Nora too. (Sure, I knew Jeff a little. Nora was a little older than me, but it would be nice to get to know her as well.)

* Nora and Jeff visit Jay often, and if I got to know them better we could all be friends.

* But if Priya and I go with Jay, we won't be able to spy on MP.
* I guess it is all right to take a break from our spying attempts.
* Everyone takes a vacation. Even spies can't work all the time.
* A good break might help Priya and me to become better spies.

I asked, "Do you want to go, Priya?"

Right away she said, "Yes!"

She certainly wanted to go.

Then I realized I had forgotten to call Mom. "We have to talk to our parents. How long will we be gone?"

"Two hours at most," Jay said.

I thought about something. "We want to come, but if we ask our parents, Kavita and Nayan will want to come too."

Jay pointed at his family's SUV. "We don't have room for them."

I looked at Priya. "Is it okay if they don't come?"

"That's fine," Priya said. "It will be easier without Nayan. I mean, Kavita sings, but he gets in other trouble."

Nora came out tucking her hair in her hat. She was talking on the phone, so we didn't say anything to her.

Jay opened the back of the SUV and put the toboggan in. There were already three helmets in the back. They must have worn them for skiing.

When Nora was done with her phone call, I said, "Hi, Nora. Could I please use your phone?"

"Sure, Nina." She handed it to me.

I called Mom's cell phone. That is also her work number, so she always answers even when she doesn't know who is calling.

"Mom, it's me. Nina," I said when she answered. "We are at Jay's house. Is it OK if Priya and I go tobogganing with them? Uncle Ryan is going to drop us off. The SUV will be full so we can't take Kavita and Nayan." I said everything out in one whoosh. I wanted her not to say anything until I explained it all, in case Kavita was listening.

"Let me ask Rita Auntie."

I held the phone and waited. I could hear some conversation in the background.

"You can go as long as you're back by lunchtime," Mom said.

"We will. Can you please open the garage door so we can take out the toboggan and the helmets?" I asked.

"Sure."

"What are Kavita and Nayan doing?"

"They are spying."

"On us?" I couldn't believe they were watching us right now from behind our fort. "Are they out there alone?"

"We can see them from the house."

My mind zigzagged with thoughts. I made an in-my-head list.

* If Kavita and Nayan were not careful, they could damage our snow fort.

* It was better not to tell them anything right now, though. That way they wouldn't know about us going tobogganing.

* And the good part about a snow fort, like a snowman, is that you can fix it easily as long as there is more snow. And we had tons of it.

* Still, I was worried that if I went to pick up the toboggan they would ask questions and find out what Priya and I were planning to do.

"Mom, what if Kavita and Nayan want to come with us?"

"I don't think they would want to. They finished your apple slices, and they are having hot cocoa with marshmallows in about five minutes. Then they need to play indoors. They can go tobogganing later."

"You didn't tell me all that."

"You never gave me a chance, Nina. Also, we only have one toboggan, so it is good that you and Priya are going now. Then Kavita and Nayan can go later. Be careful and don't be wild."

"I am never wild," I said. "Thanks, Mom."

I handed the phone to Nora. I realized that Priya and Nora didn't know each other. "This is my friend Priya," I said. "This is Jay's cousin Nora."

"How are you, Cousin Nora?" Priya said with a straight face. The way she repeated "Cousin Nora" made everyone smile.

Uncle Ryan came out. I introduced Priya to him too. "Can we stop at our house to get our stuff?" I asked.

"Of course."

He stopped the SUV by our house. Jay and I ran into the garage. Jay grabbed the toboggan, and I got the helmets. Only a week ago we had bought a new helmet for me. My old one was snug but it still fit me so now we had two. That was really lucky, because Priya could use one of them.

As Jay and I walked back to the SUV, two black-haired heads poked out over the wall of the fort.

"Did you and Priya spy on us? Like Kavita and Nayan?" Jay looked amused as if he thought that was funny. In a way it was.

"Almost-spied." I smiled.

"There is nothing *almost* about it."

I tugged at his jacket. "Let's leave quickly."

"Jay, want to come into our fort?" Kavita called.

He stopped. "I will after we get back. Have fun with Nayan!"

I put the helmets in the back. Jay hurried behind me with the tobbogan.

"Hey, how do you know my name?" Nayan shouted. "Did you spy on *us*?"

"Jay, don't spy on us, because we are spying on you," Kavita said.

"OK. Got it," Jay said over his shoulder.

Jay and I lifted the toboggan together and placed it in the back. Then he closed the door.

Nora, Priya, and Jeff sat in the very back. "Ready to roll?" Jay asked as we climbed into the middle row.

I closed the door. "Can't wait to roll down the hill."

CHAPTER EiGHT

Yay! We were on our way to Cherokee School. At least, that's what I thought. There is a big hill on one side of the school, and that's where we always go tobogganing.

"Wait!" I said. "Why are we going in the opposite direction from Cherokee School?"

Jay tapped me on the shoulder. "You know this is the way to Grandpa Joe's house."

"Aren't we going to the hill—"

"Nope. You just assumed you knew what was going on." Jay laughed. "Sometimes you do that."

"No, I don't," I said.

"Oooooh, never?"

He was mocking me. In front of his cousins. And Priya.

Jay must have seen the expression on my face. He asked, "Does it make any difference *where* we go tobogganing?"

"Yes." I gestured at Priya and then at myself. "Shouldn't our parents know where exactly we're going?"

"You're right, Nina," Uncle Ryan said. "I'll call them as soon as I drop you. Is that okay?"

Uncle Ryan was being helpful. "Yes, thank you."

"Sorry," Jay said and stared out the window. He looked glum. I think he felt bad too.

I didn't know what to say.

We were all quiet, but I didn't feel calm. Grandpa Joe's farm was only a twenty-minute drive, but it felt like we rode for two hours.

As soon as I got out of the SUV, I took in a deep breath. It made me feel a little better.

Grandpa Joe's house is on a hill, but we didn't even go inside. While we unloaded our toboggans, Uncle Ryan called Mom.

He gave me a thumbs-up after he hung up.

Maybe I shouldn't have made such a big deal about where we were going tobogganing, I thought.

Priya and I followed Nora and Jeff. Jay was behind us.

Priya squeezed my hand. "Are you OK?"

"Yes. Thank you," I mouthed the words.

Jay came up along my other side. "I'm really sorry, Nina."

I remembered how I had broken his pirate sculpture once and thought he was angry at me. I had felt bad about it and it had lasted for a long time. When I finally found out Jay wasn't mad, I had felt so relieved.

"No worries. I'm fine," I said.

He beamed. It reminded me of our snowman's smile.

Now I couldn't wait for the fun to begin.

***

We stood on the top of the hill. All around us rolling snow-covered fields glittered. I couldn't tell what was brighter, the sun or the snow. The breeze was so cool and fresh that I wanted to drink it. The snow, sun, and light breeze were exhilarating!

> **Ex-hil-a-ra-ting** means something that makes you happy and excited.

Priya gestured with her hand. "This is like a fairyland."

"It is!" Nora agreed.

"We moved from Florida, so this is all so new to me," Priya said to Nora.

"We moved to Wisconsin too, to be closer to our family." Nora swept her hand in one big motion. "I've seen snow before, but nothing like this!"

I fought a twinge of envy. This was Priya and Nora's first time seeing so much snow, and they were experiencing it together.

"Grandpa, this is Priya," Jay said when his grandfather came out.

"Welcome. Glad you're here." He turned to me. "Where's your sister, honey?"

"Kavita is at home playing with Priya's brother Nayan," I said.

"It's good that she has a friend too."

Grandpa Joe has difficulty remembering names. But that's okay. One of these days he might surprise me.

Then he went back into the house and came out with the most beautiful wooden toboggan I had ever seen.

"That's such an intricate rosemaling," I said.

"What is rosemaling?" Priya asked. "I have never heard of it."

"It's a Norwegian folk art. Our grandma's family is from Norway," Jay said.

"Over the years a lot of Norwegian families settled in Wisconsin." Grandpa Joe traced the design with his fingers. "This belonged to my wife when she was young."

"Grandpa, can we use it?" Jeff asked.

Nora shook her head. "It's special. We might ruin it."

"You won't ruin it, my child," Grandpa Joe said. "I brought it out so you can use it."

Nora carried it over and set it beside Jay's toboggan and mine. Now we had three toboggans between the five of us. I put my helmet on.

"Ready, everyone?" Jay asked.

Priya looked at me. "What do we do?"

Before I could answer, Jay said, "Ride with Nina. She's an expert."

That made me smile. "So are you, Jay."

I was lucky that I didn't have to move like Priya and Nora had. I like living in the same place. Kavita and I have our friends, and we know the same things they do. Like tobogganing and making snow angels. Like the farmers' market around the Capitol building and the Fourth of July parade. Like the Olbrich Gardens and our lakes.

Since there were only five of us and three toboggans, we each had plenty of space. I sat in front with Priya behind me on my toboggan. "Wrap your arms around me," I said.

I pushed along the ground with my hands, and it took a couple of seconds before we picked up speed. We screamed all the way down.

At the bottom of the hill, I turned around and saw that Priya's eyes were sparkling. "This is more fun than any amusement park ride."

We got out and I grabbed the rope to pull the toboggan back up the hill. "Let's do it again."

While we were trudging along, Priya said, "I'm glad Nayan didn't come. He might have been scared. Do you think Kavita would have been?"

"Probably." When we got to the top, I looked down. "This is a pretty big hill."

Jeff, Jay, and Nora caught up with us.

"One thing I know for sure," Priya said, "if Kavita were here she would start singing about the snow and the sun."

"Her very own songs, right?" Jeff said.

I tried to remember if he had ever heard Kavita burst out with her own songs. "How do you know that, Jeff?" I asked.

"Jay told me about it."

I was happy-surprised. "He did!"

"I kind of miss her. Don't you, Nina?" Jay asked.

"If you miss her singing, I can help," I said. *"Snow, snow, flow, flow from the sky. Oh, sun and snow, what a show."*

Priya tapped my shoulder. "Hey, you're pretty good. Are you sure you didn't teach Kavita?"

"No, I did not. Do you know Kavita means 'poetry' in Hindi?"

"I didn't know that," Priya said.

"Yup! So she is Miss Poetry, I'm not. Maybe I inspired her a little bit, though."

In-spire means to make someone reach for something special.

"Why do you say that?" Priya asked.

"Well, I like words, and as soon as I learn them, I try to use them. Maybe Kavita feels that since she doesn't know a lot of those words, she has to do something else. She is very smart and creative, so she makes up songs and sings them."

"To compete with you?" Jay asked. "Like you and I compete?"

"Not the same way," I said. "We compete because we're the same age and in the same class. I think Kavita works hard to have her voice heard because she is the youngest in the family."

"Is Kavita your little sister?" Nora wanted to know.

"Yes. She is a super-singer little sister," I said.

Maybe I did miss her.

Next I went on that beautiful toboggan with Jay and Priya. I closed my eyes and imagined I was a little girl from a long, long time ago. It was a special toboggan, and it was fun to daydream.

Crash!

We tumbled out. I opened my eyes. The three of us were scattered over the snow-covered ground and our toboggan had skidded far away from us. We must have hit a bump.

"Priya, you OK?" I helped her get up.

"I banged my ankle." She rubbed it. "I think I'm okay."

Jay dusted off the snow. "Sorry."

"It wasn't your fault," I said.

I should have kept my eyes open. Maybe I could have warned Jay and we could have avoided the bump. I needed to remember that careful tobogganers don't daydream. The good part was we all had our helmets on.

"Is the toboggan damaged?"

He brought it back and looked it over. "Nope."

We went down the hill again and again until my legs were too tired to climb back uphill one more time. Uncle Ryan and Grandpa Joe signaled us from a window to come in. As we took off our boots, mittens, and scarves, Uncle

Ryan brought out hot cocoa and tater tots. "They're right out of the oven, so be careful," he said.

Before leaving, we thanked Grandpa Joe. We rode home happy and floppy.

***

When we returned, Mom said Kavita and Nayan had already gone to Cherokee School with Dad and Sanjay Uncle.

"What are they going to do without the toboggan?" I asked.

"We decided to buy our own. We'll need one in Wisconsin, right?" Rita Auntie said.

Priya put her arms around her mom. "Thank you!"

After we all ate leftover pizza, Priya and I went upstairs.

She picked up Lucky and sat on my bed. "Do you have any Indian outfits?"

I showed her the one I wore at Diwali.

"The embroidery on the skirt and the blouse is beautiful." She fingered the scarf. "This is as soft as hair."

"Not my hair—mine is not very soft."

"Your hair is pretty. Don't you like it?"

"My hair is not silky like yours, and it has a mind of its own."

"You mean it's unruly. Just like you." She smiled at me.

"What does 'unruly' mean?" I asked. I know a lot of words, but I didn't know this one.

"'Unruly' means someone or something that doesn't follow any rules."

I folded my hand. "Hey, I'm not like that." I tried to pout but I think I failed.

"Maybe you're just a *little bit* unruly?"

"Opo."

She laughed. "It was fun to go to Grandpa Joe's farm. I loved standing on top of that hill and looking at the snow-covered landscape. And riding that gorgeous toboggan."

"You use a lot of big words," I said. "Just like I do."

Priya shrugged. "I like words. They are friends who understand me and help other people understand me too."

"I never thought of words as friends. I guess they are, because they do help us."

"Yes. Without words, how would I know what you want to do, how you feel about something, when you are ready to quit, and on and on. Words are great tools to have."

"So why not have as many as we can carry in our tool-boxes, I mean brains?" I said.

"Exactly." She handed me Lucky.

I put my arms around Lucky. "I like words because of the sound of them."

She looked confused. "What do you mean?"

"Well, some are fun to say, and some are challenging. Some make your brain work hard to understand them, and some make you feel peaceful."

"Give me an example of each."

Now Priya was testing me. I had found someone as interested in words as me who wanted to have a conversation about them. How utterly amazing!

Ut-ter-ly means totally.

"It's OK," Priya said. "I don't mean to put you on the spot."

"It's not that." I looked at Lucky. "Give me a minute, Priya."

"Sure."

Then she was quiet.

I said, "'Fabulous' is a fun word. 'Chivalry' is a challenging one. 'Obstacle' makes your brain work hard, and 'lullaby' makes you feel peaceful."

"Those are great examples, Nina."

"I just can't believe we are having this conversation."

"Maybe we're both weird."

"Word-weird," I said.

We both giggled.

There was something about Priya and me. We could talk and talk and talk. And the rest of the afternoon that's just what we did.

Sure, Jay is my best friend and I have known him all my life, but I enjoyed being with Priya too. We talked about clothes and hair, which I never discuss with Jay. We shared how annoying her brother and my sister can be. We both admitted that we missed them if they weren't around, though.

Is it possible to have more than one best friend? I wondered.

Maybe Jay felt the same way about Jeff. They had some special things in common. They shared Grandpa Joe and his love of fishing. Maybe Jay wanted to be friends with both of us. I shouldn't be jealous, just like he shouldn't be upset about my friendship with Priya.

I ran my fingers through Lucky's soft fur.

I understood Jay better after Priya and I talked. Jay, Nora, and Jeff didn't need to invite me. But Jay asked me and Priya to come along, because he is my friend. Jay wanted to spend time with me.

"You're quiet," Priya said.

"I was just thinking about all the fun we had today."

"Even though our spying didn't work out."

"Maybe *because* it didn't work out. If we'd stayed behind the fort, we wouldn't have gone to Grandpa Joe's farm. We wouldn't have made new friends," I said.

"We would have frozen in our fort."

"With boredom and cold." I put Lucky down. "Let's go downstairs."

As we went down the hallway, I saw something through Kavita's bedroom window. I gasped.

"What is it?" Priya asked. "MP?"

"Yup. MP's car just turned into the Crumps' driveway."

We rushed downstairs.

"You're going out again?" Rita Auntie asked as we pulled on our boots.

"We wanted to check on our snow fort," I said.

"It needs some repairs," Priya added.

Rita Auntie looked like she didn't believe Priya. "You've been out plenty. Come back inside in twenty minutes."

Priya saluted. "Aye aye, Captain Mom."

***

Priya and I crouched behind the fort and watched MP get out of the car. Priya reached for my hand. Good thing Kavita and Nayan weren't with us. They might have made noises or have been scared.

"MP is going into the garage," Priya whispered.

"MP can't get in without knowing the garage code."

The garage door opened, and MP went in.

Then MP closed the garage door.

I glanced at Priya. She put her hand over her mouth. "I wonder what MP is planning," she said.

The kitchen light was already on, but a few more came on, first in the hallway and then in a couple of other rooms.

"MP must be looking for stuff to steal," I said.

"Maybe. We should wait and see what MP takes."

"We should memorize the license plate when MP leaves. Maybe we should take a picture of the car...but we don't have a phone."

"It's difficult to spy without gadgets," Priya said.

"'Gadget'—that's one more word for our list," I said.

I wanted to run in to get Mom's phone but realized that Priya might not want to be alone while I was gone. I certainly wouldn't want to be. Plus, Mom would ask why I wanted the phone.

So we waited.

The problem with dusk is, it is not night and yet it is still spooky.

I made an in-my-head list of why dusk is not my favorite time of the day.

* It is kind of dark at dusk (even though it doesn't feel *too* dark with the snow).

* You know it is going to get darker by the minute. And the shadows are going to get scarier.

* Then comes the nighttime, which is darker than dusk. (Snow helps, though.)

* And winter nights are so long that the darkness goes on and on.

* It is also very cold in winter, especially in Wisconsin. Cold, dark, long winter nights are scary.

I shivered.

"MP seems pretty slow for a thief," Priya said.

"MP probably knows that the Crumps are gone, so there is no hurry. Or MP is looking for something special. Like secret documents."

Do-cu-ments means papers that are official and can be very valuable.

"What kind of documents?"

Priya was asking too many questions. "Like passports and driver's licenses."

"I'm sure they have their licenses with them. And they must keep their passports in a safe place. My parents do."

She pulled her hat down. "It is getting cold. We should go in."

Priya was right. It was too cold to sit in the snow fort and wait for someone when they were doing whatever they wanted in a toasty warm house.

Still, I was disappointed that we had not found out any of MP's secrets. We weren't sure if MP was a man or a woman. We had not caught MP doing anything. We needed more time. What if MP stayed in the Crumps' house all night? We certainly couldn't camp in our snow fort, waiting.

"It hasn't been twenty minutes," I said.

"Maybe not." Priya didn't sound like she wanted to stay out, though.

"If you want to, we can go in. We can spy from my room."

Then the Crumps' front lights came on. A loud noise followed.

"Look! MP is up to something," I said. "This is our chance to observe."

The garage door opened. MP wheeled out the garbage can. MP was taking a garbage can full of stuff?

MP left it at the end of the driveway, then glanced around.

"MP must be checking to see if someone is watching," I whispered.

Priya wiggled.

MP walked back to the house whistling a tune. Did MP find stealing relaxing? Maybe even peaceful?

I put my hand on Priya's shoulder. "We have to find out what MP's next move is."

"Five more minutes. Then I want to go inside," Priya said.

I wondered if Priya was afraid. I wished I had enough courage to say, "Go ahead. I will keep the post." But I didn't. If she went in, I wasn't going to be sitting out in a fort like a duck in a pond. "OK, five more minutes."

The garage door closed. Again.

This was an overnight thief-guest! MP was probably going to collect things and wait until the entire street—

maybe even the entire neighborhood and city—fell asleep. Then MP would make a move.

We waited. I don't know for how long, because we didn't have a watch or a cell phone. It felt like forever because nothing was happening. Priya squirmed. She clearly wanted to go in, so I got up and we snuck back into the house.

Winter is a good season to be quiet and sneaky. Snow doesn't make any noise when you walk on it. (Unless it melts and refreezes. Then it becomes icy and crunches.) It is also too cold to be outside for a long time. That means no one else is nearby to spot you like in the spring and summer, when people are outside and the days are long and bright. Fall can be loud for sneaking around because of all the leaves crunching underfoot. A thief would know that. Maybe that is why MP had chosen wintertime with fresh snowfall to steal from the Crumps.

Once inside, Priya and I peeled off our wintry stuff. Then we went upstairs as fast as we could. But MP had vanished!

Lots of lights had been on in the Crumps' house when we were waiting outside, but now they all were off except one, the kitchen light that had been on when MP arrived.

"Maybe MP went to bed," Priya said.

"In two minutes?" Then we heard an engine start. "Now why would anyone park in the garage, go in the house, take out the garbage, and then leave? There has to be a reason."

"Maybe MP quickly put a few precious things in the car?"

"That makes sense, Priya," I said.

"Maybe it was someone else who went out."

I hadn't thought of that. "By now the car is gone, so how do we find out for sure?"

"It's not easy to figure this out. Maybe you should just tell your parents," Priya said.

I wondered if Priya was not interested in spying any-more or if she was worried about who the MP was. No matter what, I couldn't give up. I mean what kind of a

Snow Spy would I be if I just ran to Mom and Dad before solving this mystery myself? "I don't think so. Maybe we will find out more about MP tomorrow."

We made a list in Sakhi.

> What MP is up to list
> * MP comes in to steal.
> * Takes out the garbage.
> * Hides the car in the garage.
> * Then MP probably packs the car.
> * When it is full, maybe MP drives away.
> * MP empties all the stuff in a secret stolen stash pile.
> * Then MP returns and repeats?

I read out my list to Priya. "Does this make sense?"

"Yes. MP knows the Crumps are not home, so MP has no reason to rush."

"MP probably eats all their food too," I said. "It's a pretty good deal for a thief to have things to steal, food to eat, a bed to sleep in, a shower to enjoy, and maybe even a phone to use."

"Nina, Priya," Mom called.

We went downstairs.

"Are you OK, Nina? You look flushed," Mom said.

"I am...um...fine. It's the cold."

"You came in a while ago." She touched my cheek. "Not getting sick, are you?"

My heart was pounding. "No." I licked my lips. "Maybe I am thirsty."

"Drink some water and then set the table, please," Mom said. "We will eat as soon as everyone is back."

Priya filled the water glasses and I put out the dishes and silverware.

We heard a car again and we rushed to the window. It was our car. Dad, Sanjay Uncle, Kavita, and Nayan were back. They came into the kitchen through the garage.

The phone rang. The caller ID said "Crump." How could that be? It gave me a wobbly feeling.

My heart had just settled down, but now it beat faster again.

I made a quick in-my-head list.

* Someone was calling from the Crumps' house.
* The Crumps were away and were not the ones calling.
* The only person we'd seen at the house was MP the thief-guest.
* Whoever was calling my house knew who my family was and knew our phone number.
* MP might be planning to steal from us next.
* MP was back checking on us.

My arms had goose bumps. I didn't know they were hiding under my skin until they popped up like this. I thought maybe I should do some research about how goose bumps work and where they hide.

The phone kept ringing.

"Nina, answer the phone, please." Mom was rolling rotis, and her hands were covered with flour.

Our lights were on and Dad had just driven up, so if MP was watching the house, MP must know we were home. I hesitated.

Hes-i-tate means when you're not sure you want to do something, so you take your time doing it.

While I was deciding if I wanted to answer the phone, I had more goose bumps.

All over me.

CHAPTER NINE

By the time I answered the phone, the person on the other end had hung up.

"The caller ID said 'Crump,' but they are not home. Who could it be, Mom?" I asked.

Before she could reply, the doorbell rang.

"Nina, could you please check to see who it is?" she asked. "And hurry so you don't make them wait in the cold."

I rushed to the living room and looked out the bay window. A stranger stood on our front porch. He was dressed in a pair of jeans and a red Bucky Badger sweatshirt. Bucky Badger is the University of Wisconsin-Madison mascot. He was probably a student there. He wasn't wearing a winter jacket or gloves, and he rubbed his hands together like they were cold. I'm not supposed to open the door to strangers, but maybe I could, because Mom and Dad were home. And Mom had told me to.

Before I could decide, Mom hollered, "Who is it?"

"A stranger. A man."

"I'll be right there," she said. "Please let him in."

When I opened the door slightly, the man smiled. "Soni residence?"

I took a step backward. How did he know our last name?

I nodded.

Who was he? Had he been spying on us when we were spying on MP?

Wait. Maybe I was face-to-face with MP!

Oh no! My fellow Snow Spies Priya, Kavita, and Nayan hadn't followed me to the door. Kavita is always with me when I don't need her. This time I needed her, but she had abandoned me.

> **A-ban-don** means to leave someone alone without any protection. Like leaving your friend in the rain without an umbrella.

"Come in, come in," Mom said. "You must be Noel."

I whipped around. She knew this person's name. I felt calmer.

She walked past me and threw open the door. I saw Priya peeking out from the kitchen.

He stepped in. "Yes, I'm Noel Crump. Mrs. Soni?"

"Yes. Please call me Lalita," Mom said.

I covered my mouth and made a quick in-my-head list.

* This person's last name was Crump.

* He was probably calling from the Crumps' house.

* He must be the person we saw.

* We called him MP.

* MP must be a member of the Crump family.

✳ Which means MP was not a thief at all.

✳ Or could it be that a thief named Crump was stealing from the Crumps' house?

He closed the door behind him. "I just wanted to stop by and say hello."

"Your uncle and aunt said you might spend a few days at the house."

"Yes." He glanced around. "What beautiful amaryllis you have blooming."

"Thank you!" Mom looked happy that Noel had noticed her flowers and knew their names. She said, "We're having dinner soon. Would you like to join us?"

"It smells delicious in here. But are you sure—"

"I am Suketu," Dad said as soon as he came into the living room. Noel and Dad shook hands. "Please come this way."

In the kitchen, Dad introduced Noel to everyone as Mr. Crump's nephew. Then he said, "Nina and Kavita are our daughters. Rita and Sanjay are our friends and Priya and Nayan are their children."

I wondered if Noel would remember any of our names.

I mean we only had to learn one new name and he had to learn eight! Priya glanced at me while she filled a glass of water. I put one more placemat, plate, and set of silverware on the table. The only seat left was next to me.

Everyone came to the table. Kavita sat across from Noel and stared at him. I tried to make eye contact with her. She ignored me.

Sanjay Uncle served Noel. "This is an Indian bread, roti."

"Thank you," Noel said. "I've had it at my friend's house. I love it."

Noel passed the roti box to me.

Sanjay Uncle asked, "Noel, what are you studying at school?"

"Agricultural engineering," he replied. "Even though I grew up in Milwaukee, I'm a farm boy at heart."

Mom perked up. "That's a great field."

As I handed the creamy cucumber and yogurt riata to Noel, he said, "Nice snow fort. Did you make it, Nina?"

My mind raced. Had he seen me out there? I had spied on Noel but I hadn't known that he was our neighbors' nephew. I gulped. "We...we all did," I stammered.

"My brothers and I used to make snow forts and pretend to be spies," he said.

"Oh!" I glanced at Priya. Then I tried to change the subject. I asked Noel, "Are you going to stay at your aunt and uncle's for a few more days?"

"I'm not sure. I'll return to campus tonight and see what's going on."

Kavita stared at MP.

Well, now he wasn't exactly MP, Mystery Person, because he was Noel, Mr. Crump's nephew.

"Mr. Noel, were you at the Crumps' Friday night?" Kavita's eyes narrowed.

I glared at her.

"Yes. To check the mail, Kavita," he answered. "My uncle asked me to do it."

"Nina and I saw you," she said. "Did you clean the driveway yesterday?"

Noel beamed. "Were you keeping an eye on me?"

I shrank.

"Opo," Nayan said. "Kind of."

"Well, Nayan and I tried to spy on you, but only for a while." Kavita pointed at me. "We didn't even know if you were a boy or a girl, so Nina named you MP."

I gasped. She had given up the details of almost our entire operation.

"What does MP mean?" Dad asked.

I gave Dad a look, but he ignored me.

"I forgot. Nina, what is MP?" Kavita asked.

Now all the attention focused on me. Including MP's. I mean Noel's.

Blood rushed to my face. I wished I could cover my face with a round roti.

"Nina?" Dad was giving me extra attention when I didn't want any.

"MP stands for Mystery Person," I said.

"I like the name MP," Noel said. "Did you all enjoy spying on me?"

"You didn't show up. It was boring." Kavita shook her head. "Then we tried to almost-spy on our dads."

Dad cleared his throat. "What do you mean by 'almost-spy'?"

"You spy on people because you want to find out things about them. But you're our dad and Sanjay Uncle is Priya's and Nayan's dad, so we already know everything about both of you. That is why it is called 'almost-spying.'" She looked at me proudly. "It was Nina's idea."

"Anyway, we couldn't hear you either, Dad," Nayan said. "It was no fun to wait out in the cold, so Kavita and I came in and started drawing." He pointed to Priya and me. "They stayed in the snow fort and kept on spying."

"On nobody," Kavita added.

Now Priya looked like she wanted to cover her face with a roti too.

Noel laughed. Everyone else laughed. Priya and I did not laugh.

We were caught red-handed—I mean snow-handed. Our operation had been exposed.

Ex-posed means when something is not hidden anymore, but opened up for everyone to see.

Our spying operation had become a "not-secret, everyone-knows" project.

✳✳✳

After dinner we all cleaned up, except Kavita and Nayan. They got ready for bed. Noel helped with the dishes.

"Who would have guessed MP would be standing at the sink washing riata off dishes," I whispered to Priya as I wiped the table.

Priya shook her head. "It would have been more believable if he was stealing them."

Once everything was done Noel went back to the Crumps' house. Priya and I excused ourselves and escaped to my room before anyone had a chance to ask us questions.

"That was terrible," Priya said. "I can't believe we got caught."

"At least we didn't get caught while we were spying."

Priya flopped down on my bed. "There is so much we don't know about spying. Maybe we need to attend a spy school or a spy college."

"I think we did learn something." I sat at my desk and opened Sakhi. "Let's make a list of things we learned."

I wrote down *P* next to what Priya said.

Snow Spy Lesson List

* It can be fun to spy.
* But you need someone or something to spy on. And a reason to spy on them.
* You have to dress warmly to be a Snow Spy. (P)
* You can't be afraid of the dark.
* A lot of spying is just waiting and waiting. It can get very boring. (P)
* You have to do a little extra research on your spying subject. We could have asked

Mom and Dad before and found out about Noel.

* If you plan to build a snow fort to hide behind, make sure you live in a place that gets a lot of snow. (P)

* You have to spy with the right friends who understand your plans. You can't do it with your younger sister or their friends who may be impatient or give away your secrets.

* Spying is secret, but if you suspect something dangerous, you should talk to your parents and not keep it to yourself.

I closed Sakhi. "I can't believe Kavita and Nayan gave us away."

"You should have seen your face," she said.

"I bet it looked as shocked as yours!" I said.

We both giggled.

And then we couldn't stop.

"Anyway, it wasn't all that bad," I said when there was a break in our laughing.

"It was. Admit it," Priya said.

"Spymasters, I hope you two are planning to go to bed soon," Dad said from the doorway. He was smiling. Had he been standing in the hallway spying?

"Opo," I said.

Dad came in. "What is that supposed to mean?"

Priya and I started giggling again, and this time we couldn't stop.

"Happy laughing," he said and left.

CHAPTER TEN

The next morning, Meera Masi, Uncle Ryan, and Jay came over for brunch. Nora and Jeff had gone home. Meera Masi brought idlis, which are steamed rice and lentil cakes. They were snow-soft and moon-white. Dad and Sanjay Uncle made pancakes and scrambled eggs with cheese. Priya and I helped Mom cut apples and pears. And we had some cheese curds, of course!

Delicious!

De-li-cious means something tastes very yummy.

After breakfast, Jay ran home and returned with his grandmother's beautiful toboggan.

I gasped. "When did you get this?"

"My grandpa dropped it off yesterday evening. He gave it to me."

"What about Jeff and Nora? Won't they feel bad?"

"He gave Nora a rocking chair and Jeff a toy chest with rosemaling. They also belonged to our grandma's family. So he gave me the toboggan. It's the best!"

"It's so special to have things from your grandmother," Priya said.

"It is. I never knew her, though." He looked sad.

We all turned silent.

We weren't planning to go tobogganing and we didn't have a hill, so why did Jay bring his toboggan over? Also, Jay has a regular one which is a lot easier to haul from his house to ours, so why didn't he bring that one?

I made an in-my-head list of possible reasons why Jay had brought this special toboggan over.

* Maybe he was so excited that Grandpa Joe gave it to him.

* He was sad that he didn't get to meet his grandma, so he wanted to have her rosemaling toboggan nearby.
* Since this toboggan was special, he wanted to share it with us.
* That's what friends do! Share things that are special to them.

"Hey, do you want to go for a last toboggan ride?" Jay asked Priya.

"We have to leave soon," Priya said. "We can't go far away."

I shook my head. "But there are no hills here."

"We have piles of snow," Jay said, "so we could still try."

"This time we should take Nayan and Kavita," I said.

Jay tugged at my sleeve. "Come on, let's also get your toboggan."

We headed to our garage and then outside.

We didn't put helmets on because we weren't going

down any hills. Kavita and I got on one toboggan and Priya and Nayan on the other one. Jay tried to pull us all. It didn't work well.

Sanjay Uncle came out with their luggage. "Having problems, young man?" he asked.

"Jay can huff and puff, but he can't make the toboggans move," Kavita sang.

Sanjay Uncle loaded the car. "Let me help."

Dad poked his head out of the door.

Sanjay Uncle waved to Dad. "Come on out."

The five of us sat on two toboggans and the two dads pulled us.

"That's it. Our workout for the day," Dad said after giving us the shortest ride. Ever.

"It would be nice if Jeff, Nora, and Grandpa Joe were here," I said. "We could have taken turns pulling."

"Not Grandpa Joe," Priya said.

"Oh, not for tobogganing but he would have been happy to pull us," Jay said. "He chops wood and farms. He's strong."

"I'm not saying he's weak," Priya said. "He is your grandpa, and we should give him proper respect."

"I think he would rather pull us than sit on a chair with all the proper respect piled up on him. Right, Nina?"

The way Jay asked made me realize something. It wasn't just that Jay was my best friend. I also knew his parents and his grandfather. I was also getting to know his cousins, Jeff and Nora. It made me feel special.

"For sure."

"I guess you know your Grandpa Joe best!" Priya said, then asked, "Do you realize we know a lot of people with *J*s and *N*s in their names?"

"*Jay, Jeff, and Grandpa Joe. Nora, Nina, Nayan, and Noel,*" Kavita sang. "*Oh, they all rhyme so well.*"

I didn't know Kavita was listening. Sometimes it feels like Kavita is doing her own thing, paying no attention, and then she shares her song or an opinion.

O-pin-ion means what you think about something.

"Who is Noel?" Jay asked.

Kavita sang, *"Noel is someone who loves roti, that's for sure."*

Jay looked confused but before he could say more, Nayan asked, "What about Priya and Kavita?"

"Priya and Kavita are on their own," Kavita declared.

"I will miss your singing, Kavita," Priya said.

"Maybe I will call and sing you my song about snow. It is going to be the most grand one ever."

Kavita had not forgotten about her snow song. I wondered if she had started working on it. Once Kavita has decided to do something, she does it. My sister is persistent.

Per-sis-tent means someone who keeps working or going after what they want.

∗∗∗

Priya and her family were ready to leave.

"I wish you could stay longer," I said to Priya.

She hugged me. "We'll see you in a few weeks."

"Really?"

"Yes, your parents promised me that you will all visit us before the month is over."

"I missed that! When did you ask them?"

Priya smiled. "When they were sipping their tea."

"I'm glad you asked them then. Our parents are in the best mood when they are drinking chai with friends."

"Exactly," Priya said. She turned to Jay. "I hope you can come too."

"That would be fun. Thanks for the invite," Jay said.

I called out. "Kavita, Nayan, let's take some pictures with our fort."

"I can be the photographer," Jay offered.

I borrowed Dad's phone.

Our fort glittered in the sunshine. Now that the snow had mostly fallen off the spruce branches, they looked lush and green.

"Nina and Priya, how about if you two kneel in front of Kavita and Nayan?" Jay suggested.

We did.

He took more pictures.

"How about you all go inside the snow fort and just peek over the top?"

We did that.

Jay clicked.

"OK. Now—"

"Thanks, Jay," I said. "I think we have enough. Do you want to be in a picture?"

"Sure."

We took turns posing and taking pictures with Jay.

I looked over the photos. In one of them Kavita had cut off our heads. In another, Nayan had his finger in front of the camera, so we ended up with a finger picture.

Then all the adults came outside.

Dad took our picture while we all made funny faces. That was the last one.

"It's time to go," Rita Auntie said.

I hugged Priya again. "I'm so glad you came. I had the best time." I stole a look at Jay, but he wasn't there. Kavita and Nayan were chasing him around the fort.

Jay was having a great time too.

After Priya and her family left, Meera Masi and Uncle Ryan

also went home. Jay stayed back. Kavita was so tired that she fell asleep on the living room couch. Now Jay and I had time to be together. Just the two of us.

We settled in the snow fort. The Crumps' garage door opened.

"Whose car is that?" Jay asked.

What if I don't tell him? Would Jay want to spy on the car and on Noel to find out? I wondered.

"Nina?"

"I think it's a thief. We have kept an eye on him for the last two days. He seems to take things, sleeps at the house at night, and comes and goes as he pleases."

"So you've been spying on him?"

"Yup."

Jay didn't answer. He looked through one of the holes.

I realized I didn't want to sit around watching Noel. I mean I knew who he was. I wanted to do something fun with Jay. I said, "Jay, I have spied enough for the weekend. Let's do something else, like..." I threw one of the leftover snowballs and hit him. It was easy, because he was right next to me. Then I ran. He chased me.

"Hi, Nina!" Noel waved at me.

"Hi, Noel!" I waved back. A snowball hit me. Right on my cheek.

I brushed off the snow. "Noel, this is Jay." I pointed at Jay's house down the street. "He lives in that blue house."

"Nice to meet Nina's new spy partner." Noel opened the car door.

Jay was speechless. I threw another snowball at him.

After Noel drove away, we went back to our snow fort. "OK," I said. "That was Mr. Crump's nephew. He goes to the university and is studying agricultural engineering. He grew up in Milwaukee, but he is a farm boy at heart." I went from thinking about not telling Jay anything to telling him everything. *Would a spy spill her secrets to her best friend?* I wondered. *Probably.*

His green eyes seemed to turn as bright as spruce needles. "Really? How do you know all this?"

"I am a good spy," I said.

Jay gave me a thumbs-up. "Excellent job, spymaster." For a second, he looked impressed. But then Jay shook his head. "How did you really find all this out? Kavita also sang about Noel liking roti. How did she know that? Tell me the truth, Nina." He leaned onto the fort wall, and it caved in. "I'm sorry," Jay said. "I'll fix it."

While we rebuilt the wall, I told him about how we had named Noel Mystery Person and spied on him. Then I admitted that Noel had eaten dinner with us and told us about himself. And how Kavita exposed our secret spying.

Jay laughed so hard at that part of the story that he doubled over. He crumbled part of the snow fort wall. Again!

"Stop it," I said. "It's not that funny. And you're ruining the fort."

"Sorry," he said. "But it's hilarious. You always have big plans and sometimes they turn into such a, such a..." He seemed to search for a word.

"Comical flop?" I finished for him.

"It didn't flop. Not completely, right?"

I slapped some snow on the crumbling wall. "Being a Snow Spy is not easy."

"A Snow Spy?" Jay eyed me. "Is that what you are?"

"I planned to be." I sighed. "I failed."

"No." He shook his head. "You didn't fail. Maybe froze? Or melted?"

"Maybe I'm one that's under construction."

Con-struc-tion is something that is still being worked on. It could be a building, a story, or even a Snow Spy.

✳✳✳

After Jay left, I went to my room. Dad had already taken out the extra mattress where Priya had slept. I made my bed and threw my clothes in the wash. My room looked pretty clean. Maybe picking up a little is a good idea.

I sat on my bed with Lucky on my lap.

I thought about the weekend.

I thought about making new friends.

When Priya said she wanted to be my best friend, I had stayed quiet. Jay is my best friend, but she could be my close friend too. She missed her friends in Florida, and I had made her feel better by being her friend. That made me happy too.

Maybe that's why Jay always includes Jeff. They're friends and cousins. They enjoy doing things together, like going fishing with their Grandpa Joe. That is something I don't do with Jay.

Whenever Priya visits us, we could all be friends. Four of us could do much more than just two of us. If Nora comes then there would be five of us. And Kavita would have Nayan. They would be happy too.

Sometimes you have a plan, but you end up doing something else you like even better. I wondered if spies start following one person and end up having fun with someone else. It is kind of like stumbling. You might try to go in one direction and end up going in another.

Like us.

On Friday MP came along when we weren't expecting him. We thought we would spy on people on our street, but nobody was around. Priya suggested spying on Jay, Jeff, and Nora. I wasn't sure if I wanted to do that. Anyway, once we watched them play, we forgot about spying and just joined in.

I made an in-my-head list about why we had forgotten about spying.

* How can you sit tight and spy on anyone when they are having a snowball fight?

* When they are running around having so much fun?

* When they are laughing and squealing with joy?

* You want to join them, not just watch them.

* And that is what we did!

* Then Noel surprised us.

Mom and Dad had known that Noel was Mr. and Mrs. Crump's nephew and that he was coming. When did they find out about that? Maybe I should have paid more attention to what was going on. Then I would have known about Noel.

On my desk was Sakhi, waiting for me. I shared my weekend escapade with her.

Es-ca-pade means something special you do that is a little bit naughty.

The Snow Spy Escapade

* Priya, Kavita, Nayan, and I built the fort, but we didn't have the right spy training.

* Because we hadn't attended a spy academy, we ran into problems with our methods.

* Our street is kind of quiet in the winter, so there is hardly anyone to spy on.

* We didn't spy on Jay, Jeff, and Nora like Priya wanted to. (I didn't feel right about spying on my best friend.)
* Since MP didn't come back, Priya and I took a break from spying.
* It was a fun, tobogganing outing.
* I guess sometimes a problem (not having anything to spy on) can turn into a good thing (a tobogganing adventure).
* We didn't realize we had been spying on Noel, who was in the Crumps' family.
* Noel may have been more successful spying on us than we had been spying on him.
* Still, I had found out who the MP was. I hadn't totally failed and the last three days had been thrilling.

> **Thrill-ing** means something that makes your happy
> heart race *dhuk, dhuk, dhuk.*

Still, I couldn't be a full-time spy. Not now. I have to

go to school, do my homework, and play with my friends.

Maybe someday I will attend a spy academy. But even then,

I won't spy on my parents, neighbors, or friends.

I opened Sakhi to write more.

My long-weekend list

* Making new friends
* Building a snowman
* Making snow angels
* Constructing a snow fort!
* Tobogganing with old and new friends
* Spying on a stranger
* Being surprised by the stranger, meeting him, and getting to know him
* Not being a perfect Snow Spy

Maybe I would see Nora and Jeff when they visit Jay. Maybe I would even see Noel when he came to check on the Crumps' house again.

The most exciting part was that we were invited to visit Priya and her family. That would be so much fun. Maybe when we visit them we could build other snow structures. Wouldn't it be awesome if it snowed enough so we could build an igloo?

Wait a minute! On Friday I told Jay that he thought snow was awesome because he was going skiing. That he liked the snow for what it can do for him. Like me, he probably likes snow for many reasons. Some of them have to do with all the magical qualities of snow and some with how he can have fun with it.

Jay must have figured out that I also liked snow for many reasons. He never said anything, though. I think that's because he knows me so well. No wonder he is my oldest-best friend.

I told Lucky, "Even though I wasn't a perfect Snow Spy, with the old and new friends, I had a perfect weekend."

I was born in a tropical climate. During my childhood, the temperature was occasionally low enough that I could see my breath and I would need to keep my hands in my pockets for warmth, but I did not encounter snow until I came to the United States as a teenager.

When I was six, I went on a vacation with my parents to the foothills of the Himalayas. I had heard them talk about snow-covered mountains and I was excited to see them for myself. However, all I saw was something white on the very top of the peaks, far off in the distance. It was utterly disappointing.

More than a decade later and halfway around the world, I experienced snow for the first time at Iowa State University. It was magical—white, soft, light. Dusted with snow, the brown soil and the leafless trees were transformed into a beautiful landscape. The only problem was that I was ill-prepared to trudge through snow to my classes. I didn't have the right shoes or warm enough clothing. When the snow turned to dirty slush, I was once again utterly disappointed. Then it melted and refroze, creating a layer of ice. I slipped a few times before I learned to walk on it.

Unlike me, my two daughters were born and raised in Madison, Wisconsin, where snow was a regular part of their lives. Rupa and Neha enjoyed playing outside and could handle the cold better than I had. (They also had the right kind of shoes, jackets, and gloves.)

Even though my childhood didn't include any snow, I witnessed how much fun it could be through their eyes. When Rupa was only a few months old, our neighbor, Pearl Jabs, began caring for her. After the first snow arrived, Pearl got a sled from her garage, bundled Rupa up, and took her for a walk—and she continued to do so, every single day, as long as there was snow on the ground. Pearl also taught us to how to build a snowman. My husband, my daughters, and I have made many more since then. Pearl shared stories about her childhood, growing up on a farm with her Swiss immigrant family and sledding with her many brothers and sisters.

Several of the stories from the Nina Soni series are based on my daughters' childhoods. This one is certainly inspired by their experiences. One November when they were about Nina's and Kavita's ages, we had seventeen inches of snow. School was out for days, and Rupa and Neha built a snow fort in our front yard. That entire winter, they enjoyed hiding in it, pretending to be spies. Since Wisconsin winters are long, I believe that snow fort didn't melt until May, so it provided months of fun and thrills.

The book is dedicated to Pearl Jabs, who my kids called Grandma, who was an important part of those magical snowy winters.

JAN 2023